Philip Ridley was born in the East End of London, where he still lives and works. He studied painting at St Martin's School of Art and by the time he graduated had exhibited widely throughout Europe and written his first book. As well as three books for adults, and the highly acclaimed screenplay The Krays feature film, he has written three successful stage plays: The Pitchfork Disney, The Fastest Clock in the Universe and Ghost from a Perfect Place, and two for children: Sparkleshark and Fairytaleheart. He has also written and directed two films: The Reflecting Skin – winner of eleven international awards – and The Passion of Darkly Noon. Philip Ridley has written eight other books for children: Mercedes Ice, Dakota of the White Flats, Krindlekrax (winner of the Smarties Prize and the W. H. Smith Mind-Boggling Books Award), Meteorite Spoon, Kasper in The Glitter (nominated for the 1995 Whitbread Children's Book Award), Dreamboat Zing, The Hooligan's Shampoo and Scribbleboy, which received a commendation at the NASEN Special Educational Needs Children's Book Awards 1997.

Chris Riddell lives in Brighton. He studied art at the Epsom School of Art and Design and Brighton Polytechnic. He has illustrated a wide range of children's books, including Mercedes Ice, Dakota of the White Flats, Meteorite Spoon, Kasper in The Glitter, Dreamboat Zing and Scribbleboy, and two picture books: Something Else by Kathryn Cave (shortlisted for the Smarties Prize and the Kate Greenaway Award) and Alan Durant's Angus Rides the Goods Train. He is also the political cartoonist for the Observer.

# Philip Ridley

# ZinderZunder

## Illustrated by Chris Riddell

PUFFIN BOOKS

PUFFIN BOOKS

Published by the Penguin Group
Penguin Books Ltd, 27 Wrights Lane, London W8 5TZ, England
Penguin Putnam Inc., 375 Hudson Street, New York, New York 10014, USA
Penguin Books Australia Ltd, Ringwood, Victoria, Australia
Penguin Books Canada Ltd, 10 Alcorn Avenue, Toronto, Ontario, Canada M4V 3B2
Penguin Books (NZ) Ltd, 182–190 Wairau Road, Auckland 10, New Zealand

Penguin Books Ltd, Registered Offices: Harmondsworth, Middlesex, England

First published 1998
7

Text copyright © Philip Ridley, 1998
Illustrations copyright © Chris Riddell, 1998
All rights reserved

The moral right of the author and illustrator has been asserted

Typeset in Palatino

Made and printed in England by Clays Ltd, St Ives plc

British Library Cataloguing in Publication Data
A CIP catalogue record for this book is available from the British Library

ISBN 0–140–38508–8

**For Ben Daniels –
I've always dug your razzmatazz**

## 06:03
Sunrise.

## 06:04
Light: yellow and orange.
  The sound of birds.
  And smell – flowers!

## 06:15
Slowly, Paradise Square is waking up.

What a tranquil, enchanting place it is. Especially on a beautiful spring morning like today. Daffodils, tulips and hyacinths are turning their colourful blooms towards the dawn. Butterflies and bees flutter and buzz from petal to nectar.

It's hard to believe this idyllic spot is in the centre of a city.

But look! Listen!

Tower blocks and traffic loom and pollute just beyond. But here –

Oh, Paradise Square is aptly named: a pocket of heaven in the heart of hullabaloo . . .

## 06:16

Nothing much has ever happened here.

It's a place that's never really known excitement or surprise. Some people might find that boring, of course: same routine every day, same pleasant faces, same pleasant smiles. But the people of Paradise Square . . . well, it suits them just fine.

But, today, all that is about to change . . .

## 06:23

Today there will be more excitement and surprises than most continents see in a lifetime. Let alone a tiny square in a single day.

And that's how long it all takes: a single day! Keep your eye on your watch. Within the next twenty-four hours, Paradise Square will –

But wait! Mustn't race ahead!

Let's get the story started . . .

We'll begin here. This house. See it? 14 Paradise Square. The little garden's not much more than rubble and some of the brickwork is cracked – but it's spotlessly clean and the curtains are such a delicate lace.

Look! A bedroom window's open.

Let's go inside . . .

## 06:27

Ah . . . there he is! Asleep in bed.

His name's Max Huckabee and he must be the happiest – not to mention freckliest – sleeping ten-year-old I've ever seen.

Well, you'd be happy if you were having a dream like his . . .

## 06:28

Gee whiz! Look at the people! Hundreds! No – thousands! From all over the world. All clapping. Cheering. Chanting my name over and over: 'MAX! MAX! MAX!' And look! Television cameras! My performance will be broadcast throughout the world –

Ping!

A spotlight hits me!

And look! A zillion neon lights above the stage declare: 'MAX HUCKABEE – THE GREATEST TAP-DANCER THE COSMOS HAS EVER KNOWN!'

This is it! Better start dancing –

Tap!

Tap!

Tippity-tap!

The audience shrieks with delight. Oh, I've never tapped so brilliantly –

'WAAARGHHH!'

A baby crying somewhere. Distracting me. Can't concentrate –

'WAAAARRGHHHH!'

Trip!

Slip!

Fall!

No! I'm flat on my back. And the audience is . . . laughing!

BANG! KA-POP!

No! The lights above the stage are exploding! Sparks everywhere!

'Help! HELLL –

## 06:30

'– LLLP!'

Max sits up in bed.

'WAAARGHHH!'

Gee whiz! It . . . it was just a dream. Phew! Got a bit scary by the end. Look! My pyjamas are stuck to me –

'WAAAARRGHHHH!'

Baby Fleur's crying really sets my teeth on edge.

Like fingernails down a blackboard. And – what's more – she's waking me earlier and earlier. Look! The sun's barely up. It's Saturday too. Could've had a lie-in – Wait! What am I thinking? Lie-in! That won't make me a world-famous tap-dancer. Only practice will do that. Gee whiz – perhaps I should be grateful my sister woke me! More time to practise.

## 06:31
Max jumps out of bed, puts a dab of gel on his hair (in particular the kiss-curl that swirls across his forehead), then gets dressed in (what he describes as) his 'razzmatazz image'. Although, to be honest, there's not much razzmatazz in his jeans (faded and frayed) or his T-shirt (a plain white). But his waistcoat – oh, his waistcoat – now that's a real bobby-dazzler. It's a check design. The colours? Lime green and shocking pink. You can't get more razzmatazz than that!

Because Max doesn't have proper tap-dancing shoes, he's glued beer-bottle tops to the toes and heels of an old pair of trainers. And, to make the taps sound as clear and loud as possible, he always practises on a tin tray he keeps under his bed –

Tap!
Tap!
Tap!

## 07:03
Tap!
Tap!
Tap!

'Lordy-lordy, darling! What a racket!'

The bedroom door has swung open to reveal Max's mum, Margo.

She is small, slim and wearing a neat, sky-blue dress (covered by a frilly white apron) and sky-blue stilettos (she always wears stilettos, even when doing her housework) and holding a large can of air freshener (Magnolia Dawn, her favourite). Her hair is strawberry blonde, pulled into a tight bun on top of her head and held in place by a sky-blue ribbon. Her pale skin has been powdered even paler, and her pursed mouth lipsticked bright red, so she resembles a fragile porcelain doll.

'A razzmatazz good morning to you, Mumzie!'

'A *noisy* good morning, you mean! Honestly! I do declare I thought a herd of drunken wildebeest wearing hobnail boots was playing a game of Who Can Stomp The Loudest – Argh!' Mumzie clasps a hand to her chest in shock.

'Mumzie! What's wrong?'

'Your *hair*, darling! That stupid kiss-curl! So ungentlemanly! I do declare it looks like you're practising for a Who Can Style Their Hair So It Looks Like A Squashed Worm On The Forehead competition – Argh!'

'Mumzie! What's wrong?'

'That *waistcoat*, darling! Honestly! Why must you insist on wearing such instant migraine colours? I do declare looking at you is like being poked in the eye with a vinegar-soaked chip – Argh!'

'Mumzie! What's wrong?'

'Your *shoes*, darling! Why must you wear such scruffy and –' sniff, sniff '– whiffy articles?' She sprays air freshener over Max's feet. 'I do declare they pong as much as a basket full of sweaty underpants left in the sun for a fortnight in preparation for a Smelliest Underpants In The Universe competition.'

'But, Mumzie, I need them to practise my tap-dancing –'

## 07:39

'Tap-dancing!' cries Mumzie, as if she was saying 'pus and snot smeared on my tongue'. 'Why can't you be interested in more *genteel* things, darling, instead of bouncing around like a hyperactive grasshopper with Mexican jumping beans in his socks?' Sniff, sniff. 'His *smelly* socks!' Spray, spray. 'Well, I hope you're not going to wear such vulgar things this afternoon! Have you forgotten what today is?'

'Baby Fleur's first birthday, Mumzie.'

'And what's happening this afternoon, darling?'

'Baby Fleur's birthday party, Mumzie.'

'Precisely! And Mumzie's been working so hard to make it a success! And I don't want you to ruin everything by turning up like the winner of a Look Like A Total Wally contest! Honestly, darling, you haven't been the same since you made friends with those silly old Trillian Geezers – Wait! Darling! Where are you going? Don't storm out on Mumzie like that! What have I said? Lordy-lordy!

You're upsetting Mumzie –'

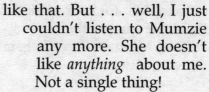

**07:41**
BOOM!

The front door slams shut.

Gee whiz! I know I shouldn't have stormed out like that. But . . . well, I just couldn't listen to Mumzie any more. She doesn't like *anything* about me. Not a single thing!

And I've asked her not to say anything nasty about the Trillian Geezers. They might be old, but they're not silly. They're my best friends. My *only* friends! It's because of the Trillian Geezers I got interested in tap-dancing in the first place.

I do wish Mumzie would see how absolutely razzmatazz tap-dancing is! But every time I start to show her what I can do, she looks the other way as if I've done something embarrassing!

### 07:42
Well – today that'll change! Today – oh, I'm trembling with excitement just thinking about it – I'm going to show Mumzie something that will make her declare, 'Lordy-lordy! What a talented tap-dancer my son is!'

The Trillian Geezers have been teaching me a special routine. It's called the Trillian Geezer All-Time Flabbergasting Pleazer. No one can resist it! Not the harshest critic! And this afternoon, at Baby Fleur's birthday party, I'm going to do it! Just a bit more practice with the Trillian Geezers and . . . oh, it'll be perfect! What's the time . . .?

### 07:44
Well, gee whiz, if I time it right the Trillian Geezers will be making breakfast when I get there. And there's nothing like a Trillian Geezer Fry-up Special for pure razzmatazz energy.

### 07:45
'Hello, ladies and gentlemen,' says Max, holding an invisible mike in front of him and staring into

an invisible TV camera, 'and may I welcome you all to *The Razzmatazz Life of Max Huckabee*.'

This is Max's favourite game: imagining it's years hence and he's hosting a documentary programme about –

'Max Huckabee! His very name means entertainment! But how did it all begin? We all know how, on that fateful spring day, Max danced at his sister's birthday party and everyone – in particular his Mumzie – realized what a genius he was! But what *led up* to that moment? In a way, ladies and gentlemen, this is the most interesting part of the story –'

**07:47**

'It all begins over here, ladies and gentlemen. 14 Paradise Square. It is in this very house that Max lived with his Mumzie. And in the beginning – long before Baby Fleur was a twinkle in anyone's eye – there were just the two of them: Max and his Mumzie. They went everywhere together. And their favourite place was Furniture Wonderland!'

**07:48**

'You can't see Furniture Wonderland from here, ladies and gentlemen. It's a twenty-minute bus ride away. But – gee whiz! – it's worth the journey. A huge building, four storeys high (plus basement), full of every kind of furniture and household appliance imaginable.

'Mumzie – she would walk round Furniture Wonderland, her eyes wide with delight. She'd run her hands over the carpets and say, "Lordy-

lordy, Little Gentleman, they're as thick as mattresses!" And when she went to the garden centre she'd say, "Oh, look at that nice, neat turf, darling!"

'But of course, Mumzie had no money. So nothing was ever bought. Her house remained carpetless and with a garden full of rubble. But oh, what fun Max and his Mumzie had at Furniture Wonderland. It was heaven, ladies and gentlemen. Pure heaven.

'One day though, this heaven was lost for ever . . .'

## 07:50

'Rain, ladies and gentlemen! Max and his Mumzie were just leaving Furniture Wonderland as the storm reached its height. "Lordy-lordy!" cried Mumzie. "I do declare I'm wetter than a hundred jellyfish in a jacuzzi! Quick, darling! Let's get into that phone box to keep dry . . . That's better! Lordy-lordy! What's this –?

*Granny Blossom's Minicabs*

*For a fragrant service*

*Telephone 87251*

'"What a genteel card! I do declare – I'm going to ring!"'

**07:53**

'Now, as you can see,
ladies and gentlemen, we've
walked further round the Square.
We're now standing outside Number 23. Granny
Blossom's Minicabs. Yes, this is the place Mumzie
phoned that rainy afternoon. And, if we look
through the window –

'There! Come closer, ladies and gentlemen.
That's the person who took Mumzie's call. Granny
Blossom. See her? Sitting at the desk. On the
phone. Just as she must have been that day when
Mumzie called for a cab. As you can see, ladies and
gentlemen, Granny Blossom's . . . well, very, very
large. And she's wearing a dress covered in the

brightest yellow sunflowers. And her hair is white and styled like . . . well, like she's just had an electric shock. And, as you can see, she's stuck a couple of flowers in it. Flowers – as you've probably guessed – are a big thing for Granny Blossom. She was born on an island in the Caribbean, you see. And all she can remember of the place is that it had lots of flowers – Gee whiz! She's put the phone down. Quick! Let's go before –'

## 07:56

'Mercy! Little Huck!' Granny Blossom dashes out of the office and points at Max. 'Tee-hee!'

'A razzmatazz good morning, Granny Blossom!'

'Oh, the things you say, Little Huck! Mercy! You make your Granny Blossom giggle and no mistake! Tee-hee! Now listen, Little Huck. Granny Blossom needs to have a serious chat with you. That was your Mumzie on the phone.' She puts her hands on her hips and sighs. 'Little Huck, I've got a sense of humour! When I see your kiss-curl – I chuckle! When I see your shoes – I chortle! When I see your waistcoat – I laugh out loud! And when I hear you're interested in tap-dancing – well, I nearly split my sides! Why? Because I appreciate a good joke!'

'It's not a joke, Granny Bloss –'

'But your Mumzie, Little Huck . . . well, God must've run out of a sense of humour when it came to making her. She takes all your tap-dancing nonsense seriously! Do you want to distress her?'

'Indeedy, no –'

'Then go back home this instant! Take off that waistcoat! Comb out that kiss-curl. Throw away those trainers! And tell your Mumzie you'll never see the Trillian Geezers –'

'It's been razzmatazz talking to you, Granny Blossom. Gee whiz, yes! But I've really got to dash –'

'Little Huck –'

'A razzmatazz goodbye, Granny Blossom!'

'Well . . . you just make sure you're not late for the party, Little Huck! You hear me? It starts at four o'clock! THE PARTY STARTS AT FOUR O'CLOCK!'

## 08:01

'Well . . . welcome back, ladies and gentlemen! Now you've met Granny Blossom. What a character, eh? Phew! And, as you can see, we've moved further round the Square. So! Back to the story of our hero, Max. Where were we? Oh, yes! In the phone box. Waiting for one of Granny Blossom's cabs . . .

'Max was holding Mumzie's hand. Her snow-white gloves were all soggy. And Max – he knew something was about to change. He didn't know what. Or how. It was just a feeling inside . . .

'And then . . . the minicab pulled up . . .

'Max couldn't see the car clearly. The rain was running down the windows of the phone box. All he could tell was . . . a man was stepping out of the car. Max pressed his face against the window. Breath misted the glass . . .

'Oh, ladies and gentlemen, Max's heart was beating so fast. He clutched his Mumzie's hand tighter and tighter. And then . . . the door to the phone box swung open and the loudest voice Max had ever heard boomed, "FRET NO MORE, DISTRESSED DAMSEL! MY NAME IS ROSCO BLOSSOM AND I'M HERE TO RESCUE YOU!"'

**08:04**

'And that, ladies and gentlemen, is how Rosco Blossom entered the lives of Max and Mumzie. Now, for those of you who have never read any of the many biographies of Max Huckabee – in particular the world best-seller *The Tap-dancer Who Changed the History of the World* – let me describe Rosco for you.

'Big, ladies and gentlemen! When Max first saw him he could have sworn Rosco was taller than the phone box. Wider too. And I don't mean fat or flab! Indeedy, no. Rosco's one hundred per cent muscle. If you were making an action movie where the hero had to fight monsters, blow up bridges and mangle helicopters with his bare hands, then you'd cast Rosco like a shot.

'"What was he wearing?" I hear you ask. Tight leather trousers, ladies and gentlemen. Black silk shirt – unbuttoned to reveal his chest (and a gold chain) – and black leather boots. And – what's more – because of the rain, everything was clinging to him, so that Mumzie had gasped, "Lordy-lordy! What a six-pack stomach!" before she had a chance to stop herself.'

**08:07**

'When they were in the car, Rosco passed Mumzie a towel. His car (a maroon Jaguar, by the way) seemed to contain everything a passenger might need: tissues, tiny bottles of drink, a comb, toothbrush, dark glasses, aspirin.

'"Well . . . thank you," said Mumzie, drying her hair. "I do declare . . . I feel quite spoilt."

'"WE ALL NEED TO BE SPOILT NOW AND AGAIN, DON'T YOU THINK, DISTRESSED DAMSEL?"

'"Oh, lordy-lordy, I do. But I implore you, don't call me Distressed Damsel any more, because just being with you has lessened my distress quite considerably. My name is Margo."

'"THERE'S SOME MAGNOLIA SCENT BESIDE YOU IF YOU'RE IN NEED, MARGO."

'"Magnolia! Why, Rosco, that's my favourite!"'

## 08:09

'Now . . . as you can see, ladies and gentlemen, we've walked around the Square a bit more now. We're at 29 Paradise Square. The Arches. So called because it's under a railway bridge and . . . well, it's shaped like an arch. And it's in that arch there – the one with the big metal doors open – that Daddy Rosco keeps his car. He waits there, when he's working, for Granny Blossom to phone through a job.

'Now, if we just peek round here a little bit . . . Ah! There he is! Polishing his car! That's all he ever does. Polish, polish, polish. If there was ever a car-polishing contest, Daddy Rosco would win it hands down. Anyway – let's creep by while Daddy Rosco's got his back to us. The last thing we want is –'

'DADDY ROSCO CAN SEE YA, SHORT STUFF! OH, DON'T LOOK SURPRISED! SAW YOUR REFLECTION IN THE MEGA-SHINY CHROME! NOW, WHY DON'T YOU GET YOURSELF OVER HERE! IT'S TIME WE HAD

SOME MAN TALK! I'VE JUST HAD A VERY DISTRESSED MUMZIE ON THE PHONE.'

**08:12**
Max is sitting in the back seat of the car with Daddy Rosco.

'SNIFF DEEP, SHORT STUFF!'

Sniiiifff!

'BOOTIFUL OR WHAT? THE WHIFF OF A FRESHLY CLEANED CAR IS THE BEST WHIFF IN THE WORLD! YOU CAN KEEP YOUR ROSE BUSHES AND ROAST BEEF! GIVE ME A CAR ANY DAY! YOU KNOW WHAT I THINK, SHORT STUFF? THEY SHOULD MAKE AN AFTER-SHAVE CALLED "CAR". AND WHEN THE MALE OF THE SPECIES SPLASHES IT ON, THE FEMALE OF THE SPECIES WILL GO CRAZY! WHAT A BEST-SELLER THAT WOULD BE, EH?'

'Mmmmm.'

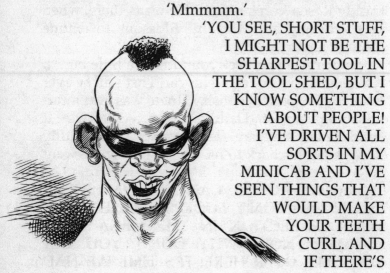

'YOU SEE, SHORT STUFF, I MIGHT NOT BE THE SHARPEST TOOL IN THE TOOL SHED, BUT I KNOW SOMETHING ABOUT PEOPLE! I'VE DRIVEN ALL SORTS IN MY MINICAB AND I'VE SEEN THINGS THAT WOULD MAKE YOUR TEETH CURL. AND IF THERE'S

ONE THINK I KNOW IT'S THIS: MEN LIKE TO SMELL LIKE CARS. IN FACT, I'VE MADE QUITE A STUDY OF THE DIFFERENCE BETWEEN THE MALE AND FEMALE OF THE SPECIES. SHALL I TELL YOU WHAT A MAN IS?'

'Mmmmm.'

'A MAN IS SOMEONE WITH MUSCLES AND A BIG CAR. HE LIKES BEER, FOOTBALL AND THICK-CRUST PIZZA. HE'S GOT HAIRS UP HIS NOSE AND IN HIS EARS. HE HATES BRIGHT CLOTHES AND FRILLY THINGS AND HIS HAIR IS SHORT. HE SITS WITH HIS LEGS OPEN. WHEN HE SEES A FRIEND HE CRIES, "WATCHYA, MATE! HOW YA DOING?" HE SNORES. HE BURPS. HE SCRATCHES HIS BUM. HE MOANS WHEN HE HAS TO GO SHOPPING –'

'But I love shopping,' interrupts Max, unable to bite his tongue and just go 'Mmmmm' any longer. 'Helping Mumzie choose a new dress is my favourite. I adore feeling the fabrics –'

## 08:15

'FABRICS!' splutters Daddy Rosco as if he's just swallowed a mouthful of vinegar. 'MEN AIN'T INTERESTED IN FABRICS! THAT'S BANG OUT OF ORDER!'

'Well, *I* am! And I don't want muscles or a big car. And I'd rather drink milk than beer any day. And football is boring! And – if I had a pizza – I'd want it *thin*-crust. And I haven't got hairs up my nose or in my ears and, if I ever did, I'd pluck them out! And I know what you're going to say next:

"WAISTCOATS ARE BANG OUT OF ORDER! KISS-CURLS ARE BANG OUT OF ORDER! TAP-DANCING IS BANG OUT OF ORDER!" Well – gee whiz, Daddy Rosco – it's been razzmatazz talking to you. But now I've really got to dash –'

'SHORT STUFF –'

'A razzmatazz goodbye, Daddy Rosco!'

'BANG OUT OF ORDER! JUST MAKE SURE YOU'RE NOT LATE FOR BABY FLEUR'S PARTY!' Daddy Rosco booms after him. 'IT STARTS AT FOUR O'CLOCK! GOT THAT, SHORT STUFF? THE PARTY STARTS AT FOUR O'CLOCK!'

**08:21**

'Welcome back, ladies and gentlemen. Now you've met Daddy Rosco. What a character, eh? Phew! Makes you realize what Max's life must have been like when his Mumzie started going out with the man. Because – oh, indeedy, yes – that's what she did. Every single night. Where they went, or what they did, Max never asked. Though a few times, Mumzie came home with popcorn in her blouse, so Max assumed they'd gone to the pictures.

'Now, I know what you're thinking, ladies and gentlemen: What was our Max doing while his Mumzie was out with Daddy Rosco? Surely he wasn't left alone? And the answer is: No. Because he stayed in that house there, ladies and gentlemen. 33 Paradise Square. And guess who lives there? Daddy Rosco's sister – Aunt Kiki!

'Oh, look at the place, ladies and gentlemen! What a mess, eh? Nearly every window is broken.

The front door's off its hinges. Bricks missing. Holes in the roof. And the garden's full of . . . well, see for yourself! An old washing machine. A mouldy sofa. And so many car tyres you'd think Aunt Kiki was entering a Who Can Keep The Most Car Tyres In Their Garden competition.

'That first night Mumzie brought Max here, he was sure she'd declare, "Lordy-lordy! This place needs a booster injection of housework!" But she didn't! She just kissed Max goodbye – oh, how she smelt of magnolia that night – and said, "Be a good Little Gentleman for your Aunt Kiki," and rushed out of the house with Daddy Rosco –'

## 08:23

Look, ladies and gentlemen! There's Aunt Kiki, coming out of the house. She's wearing her usual skin-tight leotard. Not hard for it to be skin-tight when you're as . . . well, *large* as Aunt Kiki. She's always planning to do some exercise and lose weight. But she never does. Oh, she's so scatty, ladies and gentlemen. Look! There must be at least twenty plastic brooches in her hair. And her earrings don't match (one's a plastic flower, the other's a plastic hoop) and she's only wearing one slipper – oh, quick, ladies and gentlemen! Let's get away before –'

'Coooeeee, Maxie!'

'Oh . . . a razzmatazz good morning, Aunt Kiki.'

## 08:25

'Luverducks, Maxie! Every time I see you, you're blooming dashing all over the place. Wish I had your energy! Now, your Aunt Kiki wants to have a little word with you – oooo, be careful where you step! There's a broken cup just there! Well, a mug actually. But don't let's split blooming hairs, eh? And talking of split hairs – I need to go to the hairdresser's. Want to look my best for Baby Fleur's party this afternoon. Your mum never has a hair out of place. Now – luverducks – what did I call you over for? Something to tell you. Oooo, my brain's like a pickled onion sometimes. What was it?'

'Let me guess, Aunt Kiki,' Max says as brightly as he can. 'Mumzie rang.'

'Luverducks, yes! And she wanted me to have a word with you about . . . oooo, my brain's gone again. Careful where you step, Maxie! That's either a bar of melting chocolate or some dog poo! Either way, you don't want to step in it –'

'hoooo – HAAAA!'

'Luverducks! That's your Cousin Otie! Your Mumzie spoke to him after me! Go up and have a chat with him, Maxie! He'll remember what your Mumzie wanted! Me? I'm blooming useless.'

## 08:30

'Ladies and gentlemen . . . I'm having to whisper now, because, as you can see, I'm entering Aunt Kiki's house. Now . . . we'll make our way up the stairs. Of course, you can't actually see the stairs because they're covered with so much rubbish. Tin cans. Empty crisp packets. Dirty boxer shorts. And look! There! A magazine called *Gimme Lotsa Muscles*. That should give you some idea of what my Cousin Otis – Otie, as Aunti Kiki calls him – is like.'

'HOOOO – haaaa!'

'That's him, ladies and gentlemen. You may detect a strange thing about his voice. One second it's as loud and booming as Daddy Rosco's, the next it is as feeble and squeaking as . . . well, mine. That's because Cousin Otis is a few years older than me. And his voice is – what they call – "breaking". Which means it can sound like a grown man and a boy at the same time –'

'hoooo-HAAAA!'

'Just like that, ladies and gentlemen! A squeaky "hoooo" followed by a booming "HAAAA!" – Now . . . if we just peek through the banisters –

There! You see? That's Cousin Otis. Look at him! Standing in the middle of his bedroom, wearing nothing but black boxer shorts and . . . well, muscles. In other words, a smaller version of Daddy Rosco. He's doing his weight-training! Every time he lifts the weights he goes "hoooo-haaaa" – Gee whiz! Look at his veins bulge. He's going to explode if he's not careful –'

'THAT you CREEping abOUT out THERE, MaXIE-weED?'

'Oh . . . a razzmatazz good morning to you, Cous –'

**08:34**
'NOW you CAN quit ALL that RAZZmatAZZ balONey, MAXie-WEed. It's TIME you AND me HAD A litTLE man TO mAN CHat! Or SHOuld I SAY, man TO weED? LoOK at YOU, MAXie-WEed! THAT nerdy KISS-curl! THOse NERdy SHOes that SMell woRSE than MY swEATY armPITS! And AS for THAT WAISTcoat! I JUST doN'T DIG it! YOU UNDersTAND WHat I'm SAYing? I DOn't DIG it! AND NO one with aNY sENSe DIGS it EIther!'

'Well, gee whiz, Cousin Otis, I know this ain't your style, but –'

'Not MY style, MAxie-WEed! It's NOT anyONE's style. NOT a male MEMber OF the SPEcies AT any RATE. It's the STYle of a wiMP. A NERD! A GEEK! ThAT'S whAT you ARE, maXIE-weED. A GEek! And IT'S got TO stop! BECause YOU'RE emBARRASSing your POOR Mumzie. SHE JUST DON'T DIG YOU!'

'Well, thank you for your advice, Cousin Otis,' says Max as brightly and cheerfully as he can manage. 'And – gee whiz – it's been a pure joy chatting to you. But now I've really got to dash –'

'maxIE-weEED –'

'A razzmatazz goodbye, Cousin Otis!'

'YOU just MAke SUre YOU're NOT LAte for BAby FLEur's PARty, MAXie-weED! IT STarts AT FOur o'CLOck! HEar THat? THE parTY STArts at FOur o'cloCK!'

**08:38**

'Welcome back, ladies and gentlemen. Now . . . I know what you're thinking: Didn't Max *tell* his Mumzie? Didn't he *plead* with her, "Don't go out tonight, Mumzie! I can't bear staying at Aunt Kiki's! Cousin Otis makes my life hell!" Well, the answer is: No, ladies and gentlemen. He didn't. And why? Because . . . his Mumzie looked so happy. Happier than Max had ever seen her before. So . . . our Max kept quiet.

'And then, one night, Mumzie came back from her night out – more popcorn than ever in her blouse – and announced, "Lordy-lordy, have I got a big surprise for you, Little Gentleman. You're going to have a tiny friend."

'"What do you mean, Mumzie?"

'"A brother or sister is what I mean."

'"I . . . I don't understand, Mumzie."

'"Lordy-lordy! I do declare sometimes you're as dim as a box of broken light bulbs being sucked into a black hole. Darling . . . Mumzie's going to have a baby!"'

## 08:39

'A baby, ladies and gentlemen! The word buzzed inside Max's head like . . . like a wasp in an empty Coke bottle! Baby! Baby! Baby!'

## 08:40

'And now . . . now we move forward in our story, ladies and gentlemen. It is the day of Baby Fleur's birth. Imagine this: A hospital corridor. Sparkling white tiles everywhere. The smell of antiseptic. Everything echoing. And there . . . there's Max! Sitting all alone. He looks very distressed. And for good reason. His Mumzie's in the room at the end of the corridor . . . Oh, ladies and gentlemen, I can see it all. So clearly. Like it's a scene from a movie . . .'

## 08:41

What's going on down there? thinks Max. They're all in there with Mumzie – Daddy Rosco, Granny Blossom, Aunt Kiki! One of them should come out and tell me what's going on. Don't they realize I'm worried? It's *my* Mumzie in there!

'What have we here, Brother Little Trill?'

'A most unrazzmatazz fellow, Brother Big Trill.'

Gee whiz! They took me by surprise! It's the . . . oh, what are their names? They live in the Square. The twins! They used to be on the stage or something. Years ago. They must be about seventy years old now. Ancient! Everyone in the Square thinks they're a bit of a joke really. And – gee whiz! – they certainly dress like jokes. Look at them! Both wearing identical waistcoats. And lime-green and shocking-pink check waistcoats at that! And their hair – I suppose it was ginger once. But now it's faded to . . . bright yellow! And they've lost most of it. Just a little bit on either side. And a curl that starts at the back of their head and stretches to their forehead. A kiss-curl, I think it's called. And yet . . . they have such kind, warm faces. And the way they're smiling at me. Makes me want to smile right back.

'Oh . . . hello. I'm sorry . . . but I seem to have forgotten your names!'

'Well, bless my soul, there's no reason why you should remember. After all, we're not famous any more. Right, Brother Little Trill?'

'Indeedy, yes, Brother Big Trill.'

'Our day has long since faded, my little fellow. But once . . . once we blazed, fierce as a comet across the showbiz sky. But – like all comets – we have shot out

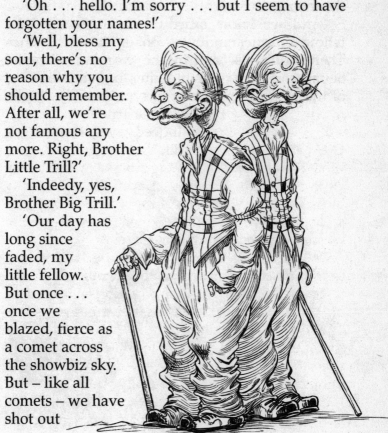

into the vast oblivion of whatever-happened-to. Please allow me to introduce ourselves. We are the Trillian Geezers!'

## 08:45

'The Trillian Geezers!' cries Max. 'That's it! Big Trill and Little Trill – because one's seven minutes older than the other! Gee whiz! I'm sorry I forgot . . . but, well, I've got a lot on my mind at the moment.'

'And we know exactly what it is, my little fellow. Your dear mother – Oh, don't look like that. There are no secrets in the world of Paradise Square. And we've got nothing to do but look out of the window and be as nosy as possible. Right, Brother Little Trill?'

'Indeedy, yes, Brother Big Trill.'

'Although some days – like today – we stop being nosy and visit this place to try and cheer people up. Older people, usually. The ones who remember us from our heydays. I'll tell you what, my little fellow. We'll cheer *you* up! Right now! Heavens to Betsy, yes! Prepare yourself, little fellow. You are about to be entertained by the Trillian Geezers the Walloping Caesars! Ready, Brother Little Trill?'

'Always, Brother Big Trill.'

And then . . .

Tap! Tap!

Tap! Tap!

Tippity! Tippity –

## 08:47

Look at their feet! Tapping away! The sound's echoing up and down the corridor. All around me. Inside my skull. Inside my belly. I never knew feet could make such glorious noises –

Tap! Tap!

Tap! Tap!

Tippity-tap! Tippity-tap –

Other people are watching now! A couple of nurses! Someone in a wheelchair. Doctors! And they're all smiling! Enjoying it! Oh yes! Yes! Dance on, Trillian Geezers! Dance on! Dance –

## 08:49

'SHORT STUFF!'

Wh . . . what's that? Oh – it's Daddy Rosco! He's calling me from the end of the corridor.

'COME HERE, SHORT STUFF! QUICK!'

The Trillian Geezers have stopped dancing.

The crowd is dispersing.

'Be right there, Daddy Rosco – Oh, thank you, Trillian Geezers! That was so . . . so . . .'

'Razzmatazz, little fellow! That's what it was! And if you're ever in need of more razzmatazz, then . . . well, you know where we live. 37a Paradise Square. You can visit us any time! Can't he, Brother Little Trill?'

'Indeedy, yes, Brother Big Trill.'

## 08:50

I'm walking down the corridor now. Daddy Rosco is smiling so wide! He puts his arm round my shoulders. He hugs me. First time he's ever done that.

'THE BABY'S BOOTIFUL, SHORT STUFF!'

We go through a door . . . There's Granny Blossom. And Aunt Kiki. They're both smiling at me . . . And there's Mumzie! Sitting up in bed. And she's . . . holding something! It's small. Wrapped in a blanket. Going –

'WAAARGH!'

Granny Blossom says, 'Mercy! She's a flower and no mistake.'

And Aunt Kiki says, 'Luverducks! She's fan-blooming-tastic!'

And Daddy Rosco keeps saying, 'BOOTIFUL!'

And Mumzie says, 'Her name's Fleur, darling! Such a genteel name! So refined! Well – what do you think of your sister?'

I think . . . I think she's noisy. I think she needs more hair. I think she needs teeth. I think . . . I think I want to get away from this noisy, hairless, toothless thing –

**08:55**

'And, ladies and gentlemen, that's exactly what Max did. He got away. And can you guess where he went? Exactly! 37a Paradise Square. The house of the Trillian Geezers! And that's where we're going now! Come on! Quick!

'That's their house . . . See it? Painted with lime-green and shocking-pink squares! The Trillian Geezers' trademark! I'm ringing the doorbell . . .'

DA-DING! DA-DONG!

'TRILLIAN GEEZERS! YOUR WONDERMAX IS HERE!'

**08:58**

'WonderMax!' cries Big Trill, giving Max a big hug. 'A most razzmatazz good morning to you, my precious fellow. Heavens to Betsy! What a sight for my old eyes you are. Oh, enter, WonderMax! Enter our humble abode! Brother Little Trill! Stop frying bacon and see who's come to join us!'

'WonderMax!' cries Little Trill, coming out of the kitchen, clutching a frying pan. 'A most razzmatazz good morning to you, my precious fellow! You're just in time for a Trillian Geezer Fry-up Special!'

'Sounds razzmatazz!' says Max, flopping into an armchair.

**09:00**

This is my favourite place in the whole world,

thinks Max. The Trillian Geezers' house is cram-packed with razzmatazz things: posters of stage and film musicals; photographs of all sorts of dancers from all sorts of places. Some of the photos are very old, faded black and white, with edges all yellow and curling. But others . . . oh, others are glossy and new, as bright and colourful as stained-glass windows. And there's framed old press cuttings too. One of them says: LOCAL TWINS TAP-DANCE TO VICTORY.

It's hard to believe – when the Trillian Geezers were about my age, nearly every country in the world was fighting. It was the Second World War. Bombs were dropping all over the place – including Paradise Square. And – through it all – the Trillian Geezers wore their razzmatazz waistcoats and danced. In air-raid shelters at night (and amongst ruins the following morning) they tapped to take people's minds off the nightmare. Look! There's a photo of them. Dancing amongst the rubble! Oh – gee whiz – how brave they were –

'Fried bread, WonderMax?'

'Indeedy, yes, Big Trill.'

'And mushrooms, WonderMax?'

'Indeedy, yes, Little Trill.'

And look! The room's full of old theatre props and costumes. I particularly like that hat decorated with plastic fruit! And as for the furniture . . . well, the seat I'm sitting on is a throne from a play about Cleopatra. And the chandelier above, that's from . . . well, something very posh and grand –

'Bacon done crispy, WonderMax?'

'Indeedy, yes please, Big Trill.'

'And a sweet cup of tea?'

'Indeedy, yes please, Little Trill.'

And look! There! They've built their own mini-stage in the corner of the room. Complete with spotlights and curtains. If I lived here, I could tap-dance all I wanted –

'Breakfast, WonderMax!'

'Breakfast, WonderMax!'

**09:07**

'Mmmmm . . . razzmatazz fried bread, Big Trill!'

'Thank you, WonderMax.'

'And the tea always tastes better in these old goblets, Little Trill.'

'Good golly Miss Molly, yes, WonderMax! They're from an old production of *Robin Hood and His Merry Men*, I seem to remember. Although, if you don't mind me saying, WonderMax, you're not looking particularly merry this morning. Is the bacon too crispy for you, my precious fellow?'

'Oh, gee whiz, it's not the bacon! The bacon – in fact, the entire breakfast – is pure razzmatazz. It's just that – oh, I've had a pretty tough morning. First Mumzie, then Granny Blossom, then Daddy

Rosco, then Aunt Kiki and Cousin Otis – not one of them understands my razzmatazz.'

'Heavens to Betsy, my precious fellow,' cries Big Trill, nearly choking on a mushroom, 'you mustn't let other people's ignorance get you down. You  know our motto: Be true to your razzmatazz! No matter how much an audience might boo or throw rotten vegetables –'

'But I wouldn't mind it if an audience booed, Big Trill. Or threw vegetables. I don't need a huge audience to like me. I just need . . . Mumzie. That's not too much to ask, is it?'

'It's not too much at all,' sighs Big Trill, giving Max's shoulder an affectionate squeeze. 'But . . . well, the things you're interested in, my precious fellow, are *different*. Heavens to Betsy! It's these different things that *make* you special. But you pay a price for being special. And that price is, people taking the mickey out of you. In fact, everything you consider to be razzmatazz, others think funny or weird. And, sometimes, people like us pay the biggest price of all: when someone we love – in this case, your Mumzie – fails to see our razzmatazz.' Then, taking a big slurp of tea, he continues, 'But, of course, what you have to realize, my dear WonderMax, is that most people suffer from the BJLM disease.'

**09:10**
'What's the BJLM disease, Big Trill?'

'Be Just Like Me! Most people are in the chronic stages of this terrible virus. As soon as they see someone who's *not* Just Like Them, they have a horrific reaction. They point. They laugh. They call funny names. Oh – heavens to Betsy – what a shocking illness it is! You have to feel sorry for these people. Right, Brother Little Trill?'

'Good golly Miss Molly, yes!'

'And you, my dear WonderMax, you have to be strong in the face of BJLM sufferers. You must think of all the razzmatazz folk who went before you, who suffered similar things. And you must say those magic words that misunderstood razzmatazzers have yelled at BJLM sufferers since showbiz began.'

'What words?'

Both Big Trill and Little Trill take a deep breath and yell, 'YAH BOO SUCKS!'

**09:12**
'Gee whiz!' gasps Max in surprise (and unable to suppress a little chuckle). 'I couldn't say that to Mumzie! You know what she's like. Only last week I let a "blooming" slip out and Mumzie nearly had a heart attack. "Lordy-lordy," she cried, "I do declare you sound like you're practising for a Who

Can Speak The Most Uncouth Things competition."' Then Max sighs and, idly dipping some bread into egg yolk, says, 'It's hard for us showbiz types when your Mumzie's your harshest critic.'

'Critic!' gasps Big Trill. 'Heavens to Betsy, my precious WonderMax, that's the most insulting thing you can call anyone! You mustn't call your slimiest, nastiest, creepiest enemy a critic, let alone your Mumzie! Right, Brother Little Trill?'

'Good golly Miss Molly, yes, Brother Big Trill!'

'But – Big 'n' Little Trills – she finds fault with *everything* I do. Nothing pleases her. Gee whiz – I bet she won't even like the Trillian Geezer All-Time Flabbergasting Pleazer!'

'Impossible, WonderMax.'

'Impossible, WonderMax.'

'Oh, I'm not so sure, Big 'n' Little Trills! Perhaps I'll start dancing at the birthday party – as planned – and all Mumzie'll say is, "Lordy-lordy, darling, take off those whiffy shoes."'

## 09:15

'WonderMax!' cries Big Trill, wiping his hands on the tablecloth (a particularly frilly item from a production about the French Revolution). 'You mustn't talk like this! Negative thoughts are not allowed in this house. Only positive! And I tell you this – oh, heavens to Betsy! I'm getting so excited, look at me tremble – you *will* perform the Trillian Geezer All-Time Flabbergasting Pleazer this afternoon. And you *will* be a huge success! And your Mumzie will *not* mention your whiffy shoes, because – oh, Brother Little Trill, I can't contain myself any longer. I'm going to have to give it to him now!' Big Trill rushes to a cupboard and removes a box wrapped in lime-green and shocking-pink wrapping paper. 'A gift, my precious WonderMax,' he declares, thrusting it at Max. 'From Brother Little Trill and me!'

'A g-gift! For me? Wh-why?'

'Why?' cries Big Trill. 'What do you mean, why? Because you're our own special, precious WonderMax. Because . . . since you started visiting us, our whole lives have changed. You've made us feel razzmatazz again. And because . . . oh, WonderMax, just open the present! Open! Open!'

Gee whiz! What can it be? Not very big. About the size of a shoebox – No! It can't be! It just can't –

Ripping paper!

'TAP-DANCING SHOES!' cries Max.

**09:21**

The shoes are – needless to say – covered in lime-green and shocking-pink squares, with bits of metal nailed to the heels and toes.

'Oh, Big 'n' Little Trills! I can't thank you enough! Look at them! Tap-dancing shoes! I . . . don't know what to say –'

'Don't say anything, my precious WonderMax,' declares Big Trill, grinning with joy. 'Just put them on.'

'Gee whiz! I will . . . Look! They fit me perfectly! I've got to dance! Now!'

'Then dance you shall! Up on that stage, dear

WonderMax.'

Max rushes to the stage and –
TAP!
TAP!
TAP!

'Listen to that, Big 'n' Little Trills! So loud! So clear! Especially on this stage! So . . . so pure razzmatazz!'

'Heavens to Betsy, yes, WonderMax!'

'Good golly Miss Molly, yes, WonderMax!'

'And – oh, gee whiz! You're right, Big 'n' Little Trills. In these shoes . . . . Mumzie can't fail to be impressed when I dance! So now . . . oh, let's practise! Practise! Practise! Practise!'

## 09:30

Big and Little Trills have pulled two chairs (high-backed things from some Shakespearian production) close to the stage and are instructing Max in the finer points of the Trillian Geezer All-Time Flabbergasting Pleazer.

'Keep the tempo, WonderMax. Five, six, seven, eight!'

'And keep smiling, WonderMax!'

'Energy, WonderMax!'

'Rhythm, WonderMax!'

**10:30**
TAP!
  TAP!
  TAP!
  TIPPITY!
  SPIN! TAP! TAP!
  'Now double back, WonderMax!'
  'Repeat it, WonderMax!'

**11:30**
TAP!
  TAP!
  TAP!
  TIPPITY! SPIN! TAP!
  'Click your heels, WonderMax!'
  'Click, click, WonderMax!'
  'Again, WonderMax!'
  'Again, WonderMax!'

**12:30**
CLICK!
  TAP!
  TAP!
  TIPPITY!
  SPIN! TAP! TIPPITY!
  'Getting better, WonderMax!'
  'Much better, WonderMax!'

**13:00**
'It's one o'clock, WonderMax! Let's break for some lunch.'

  'But, Big Trill, I don't want to waste time eating! I want to practise –'

'Heavens to Betsy, WonderMax, you must get some sustenance inside you! You can't wallop those feet successfully on an empty stomach! Besides, my belly's rumbling so loud I can barely hear you. Brother Little Trill – one of your salmon and cucumber sandwiches, if you please.'

## 13:30
'Salmon fresh enough for you, WonderMax?'
    'Indeedy, yes, Big Trill.'
    'And the cucumber, WonderMax?'
    'Indeedy, yes, Little Trill. But –' munch, munch '– I want to start practising again as soon as possible!'

## 14:30
TAP!
    TAP!
    'Better all the time, WonderMax!'
    'Better all the time, WonderMax!'

## 15:30
TAP!
    TAP!
    'Nearly there, WonderMax!'
    'Nearly there!'

## 16:01
'STOP!' Big Trill jumps to his feet and claps his hands excitedly. 'Oh, be still, my beating heart! Brother Little Trill, have you just seen what I've just seen?'
    'Good golly Miss Molly, I do believe I have,

Brother Big Trill.' Little Trill is on his feet as well, clapping every bit as much as his brother.

'Gee whiz! Wh-what have you seen, Big 'n' Little Trills?'

'WonderMax, my precious fellow, Brother Little Trill and I have just witnessed the most perfect, the most outstanding, the purest razzmatazz performance of the Trillian Geezer All-Time Flabbergasting Pleazer since . . . well, since we – the Trillian Geezers the Walloping Caesars ourselves – first performed it many years ago! WonderMax, make no mistake, you have just tap-danced a masterpiece to rival the greatest dances in history. Why, if the legendary Salome – yes, Salome herself – were here, she'd fall to her knees and lick the jam from between your toes, crying, "My Dance of the Seven Veils is but the graceless galumphing of an intoxicated camel compared to your poise and skill" – Oh, WonderMax! My boy! My genius! How proud you make us! My cup runneth over! – Bravo, WonderMax! Bravo!'

'Bravo, WonderMax!'

And, tears streaming down their faces, Big Trill and Little Trill jump up on to the stage and embrace Max and kiss him on both cheeks.

'Gee whiz! I *knew* it was good! I could *feel* it! Inside! Oh, I – gee whiz – I feel like I've got pure razzmatazz pumping through my veins. It's like . . . like a power. Oh, it was worth all the hours of practice – hours! Wait! What's the time?'

## 16:07
'GEEEEEWHIIIIIZZZZZ!'

'What's wrong, WonderMax?'

'You've gone quite pale, WonderMax!'

'I'm late! For the party! It started at four o'clock! Seven minutes ago! Oh no! Mumzie will never forgive me. I've got to dash! Thank you again, Big 'n' Little Trills! A razzmatazz goodbye!'

And, with that, Max runs out into the Square and –

**16:09**

– past Aunt Kiki's house

**16:10**

– past the Arches

**16:11**

– past Granny Blossom's Minicabs . . .

**16:12**

'MUMZIE! I'M HOME!'

'Lordy-lordy! Look at the time!'

'I'm sorry, Mumzie, but I – I –'

'Every time you visit the Trillian Geezers you forget all about your poor Mumzie. But today of all days! It's quite unforgivable. I've been rushing around faster than a whirling dervish in a Drink Twenty Cups Of Coffee And Whirl As Fast As Possible competition. I've had to do everything myself! Well . . . we'll talk about that later. I'm not going to let you ruin my day. We're having the party in the garden. I heard ladies of refinement favour outdoor dos. Everyone else is here. *They* were on time. Go out and say hello.'

'A razzmatazz hello, everyone!'

'You're late, Little Huck.'

'BANG OUT OF ORDER, SHORT STUFF!'

'Luverducks! Your poor Mumzie's been frantic, Maxie!'

'baNG out OF ORder, MAXie-WEed!'

'Sorry, everyone! But – gee whiz – I've been practising something and I can't wait . . .'

No one's really listening. They're all clustered round Baby Fleur. Look at her. On that blanket. Dressed in the frilliest, pinkest outfit I've ever seen –

'Mercy! Look at her!'

'BOOTIFUL!'

'Luverducks! Blooming lovely!'

'bootIFUL!'

Daddy Rosco's wearing so much aftershave I can smell it from here. The way he's kissing Baby Fleur and grinning you'd think he was entering a Kissing 'n' Grinning contest. Aunt Kiki's idea of dressing up is to wear larger earrings. And – needless to say – they don't match. And Cousin Otis – as usual – is doing anything to suck up to Daddy Rosco. Look at him! Wearing exactly the same clothes. What a joke!

It's a shame some of the sunflowers on Granny Blossom's dress aren't in the garden. Mumzie's tried to make it look as neat as possible, but it's still nothing but rubble! Wait a minute! That slab of concrete. That'll be a perfect place for me to perform the Trillian Geezer All-Time Flabb –

**16:22**

'I'M SO GLAD YOU COULD ALL COME TO CELEBRATE THE FIRST BIRTHDAY OF THE MOST BOOTIFUL LITTLE GIRL IN THE WHOLE WIDE WORLD –'

Mumzie's given drinks to everyone and Daddy Rosco's making a speech now. Listen to him! He'll go on and on like this for ages. As for me . . . I'm getting really excited. Butterflies in my belly. Hundreds of them. Thousands! But it's a good feeling. Oh, I can't wait for everyone to see me dance –

'– SHE'LL GROW TO BE A PERFECT LADY! SHALL I TELL YOU WHAT A LADY IS? A LADY IS SOMEONE WITHOUT MUSCLES AND WHO DON'T DRIVE! SHE LIKES LEMONADE, ICE-SKATING AND THIN-CRUST PIZZA –'

Gee whiz! Listen to him! But – just wait till he sees me dance. He'll soon change his mind –

'A TOAST! TO BABY FLEUR!'

'Mercy! Baby Fleur!'

'Luverducks! Baby Fleur!'

'wooo-HAAA! BaBY fleUR!'

'Lordy-lordy – Argh!'

'Mumzie! What is it?'

**16:27**

'Your shoes, darling!

---

— 44 —

Lordy-lordy! They're the most . . . *ungentlemanly* things I've ever seen! Look at them! It's like someone's been sick over your feet! And – argh – the colours! Honestly! I think they've done serious damage to my retinas! Protect Baby Fleur's eyes, someone! Oh, today of all days, darling! You've done it on purpose! Anything to . . . to ruin your little sister's day! What a selfish, jealous boy you are!' And suddenly, tears spring to her eyes and she's rushing into Daddy Rosco's arms. 'Oh, what am I going to do with him, Daddy Rosco?'

Daddy Rosco strokes Mumzie's hair and kisses her gently. 'DO NOT DISTRESS YOURSELF, PRETTY LADY.' Then he glares at Max. 'YOU'RE BANG OUT OF ORDER, SHORT STUFF!'

'But . . . oh, gee whiz! The shoes – they're a present! From the Trillian Geezers –'

'Lordy-lordy!' shrieks Mumzie. 'If I hear those silly old fools' names one more time I'll scream! They've turned my one-time Little Gentleman into a laughing stock! Honestly! What will the neighbours think? – Oh, Granny Blossom! Granny Blossom!'

'Mercy! Don't upset yourself!' And now Granny Blossom is wrapping her arms round Mumzie. 'You naughty boy, Little Huck!'

'Naughty! But – gee whiz! – I don't mean to be. I only want to dance –'

'Dance?' shrieks Mumzie, wiping her tears on Daddy Rosco's shirt. 'Oh, Aunt Kiki! Cousin Otis!'

'Luverducks! Don't be blooming upset!'

'do NOT distRESS yourself, AUNTie MARgo!'

Gee whiz! This is just like Mumzie! She's

managed to get everyone on her side. Look at them. Clustered round her. All glaring at me like I'm Public Enemy Number One. Well . . . I'm gonna change that. Once and for all!

I'm going to dance!

NOW!

## 16:31

Where's the concrete?

Here!

Jump on!

Take a deep breath. And –

Tap!

Tap!

Tippity –

## 16:33

Mumzie looks up as if she's about to tell me to stop. But – she doesn't! Look at her. She's just frozen! Transfixed. Oh – gee whiz! – It's working! The Trillian Geezer All-Time Flabbergasting Pleazer is working!

Tap!

Tap!

Tippity!

Spin!

Click!

Tippity –

Now Daddy Rosco looks!

He's transfixed too!

Tap!

Tap!

Click! Spin! Tap –

Now Granny Blossom stares!
She's transfixed too!
Tap!
Tippity! Click! Spin –
Aunt Kiki stares.
Transfixed.
Tap!
Tap!
Cousin Otis stares.
Transfixed.
Tap!
Tap!

**16:34**
Everyone's staring! Their eyes full of wonder!
And me – oh, I'm dancing! Dancing better than ever. The taps are as sharp as firecrackers. Pure razzmatazz! This is the greatest moment of my life! The greatest!
Tap!
Tap!
Tippity! Click! Click!
Click! Tap! Spin! Tap!

**16:36**
'THERE!' cries Max, striking the final pose.
'Lordy-lordy!' gasps Mumzie.
'Mercy!' gasps Granny Blossom.
'BOOTIFUL!' cries Daddy Rosco.
'Luverducks!' cries Aunt Kiki.
'bootIFUL!' cries Cousin Otis.
'Oh – gee whiz – everyone,' says Max breathlessly. 'I *knew*! I just *knew* you'd like it –'

'Not you, darling!' Mumzie snaps. 'Baby Fleur! Look! She's walking!'

**16:37**
Everyone's dashing straight past me.

They're going to Baby Fleur.

And – yes, look! – Baby Fleur is taking a few tentative steps.

'Walking! Oh, lordy-lordy!'

'BOOTIFUL BABY!'

'Mercy! At last! Walking!'

'Luverducks!'

'I dIG iT!'

I-I can't believe it! Wh-what about me? My dancing!

Oh . . . I've got to get out of here –

**16:39**
BOOM!

The front door slams.

Wind!

Out of nowhere, a wind disturbs the tranquillity of Paradise Square. Litter blows across the street. Trees bend and creak. An explosion of pink blossom clouds the turbulent air.

SSSCHWEEE!

Max marches across the Square. Not knowing where he's going. Just walking! Walking for the sake of walking.

Walking into the violent wind –

**16:42**
SSSSCHWEEE!

Now the air is full of flowers as well.
Daffodils.
Crocuses.
Tulips.
Hyacinths.
A multicoloured cyclone swirls and whirls.
And that's when a sheet of paper blows into Max's face –

## 16:45
Get off! Must be one of those flyers for jumble sales or something. Get off! Get off –
Max pulls it away!
Chucks it!
SSSSSCHWEEEEE!

Back into his face!

Gee whiz! What's wrong with this thing? Get off!

Max pulls it away again.

Chuck!

He walks down to the canal.

**16:49**

Max is calming down now.

And the wind is fading too. Going as quickly as it came. No blossom or flowers in the air. No sound of things falling over. Just –

Splash!

What's that? Look! Something jumping in and out of the canal! Must be a fish! Didn't think there were any fish left – Wait! It's not a fish! It's –

Shmack!

The sheet of paper jumps out of the water and sticks to Max's face.

What's going on? Gee whiz! Let's peel it off!

Peeeeelll!

It's sticky! And . . . well, how can a piece of paper jump in and out of the water like that? If I didn't know any better, I'd think it was following me –

The paper wriggles in Max's hands.

**16:51**

'GEE WHIZ!'

Max throws the paper to the ground.

Takes a step back –

The paper follows – Rustle!

'GEE WHIZ!'

Step back.

Rustle!

Back.

Rustle!

'Wh-what do you want?'

And with that, the paper leaps back into Max's hands.

## 16:54

'GEEEEE WHIIIIZZZZZ!'

Get it off! What's going on? This is crazy – But wait. What's this? There's something written on it –

## 16:55

*Dear None Too Happy Young Person,*

*This sheet of paper – known as a Zinder-Zundergram – has been attracted by your None-Too-Happiness.*

*I'm sorry that your happiness level is not all it should be – but fear not! I am here to help!*

*Or rather, the ZinderZundergram is here to tell you how I can help.*

*My name is ZinderZunder. (And by the way, that's not a grammatical error – that's how it's supposed to be written. One word, but with two capital Zs.) I live very, very far away in a place called ZinderZundia. It's quite charming. I'm sure you'd like it if you came for a visit –*

*OK! OK! I know what you're thinking! Get on with it. So the deal is this: I can give you what you want! Simple as that!*

*All you have to do is tell me what it is!*

*Now, I know what you're thinking! How can I tell you? Simple! The telephone! And, what's better, you don't even need a number.*

*Just say my name into the phone with every bit of passion in your heart and you'll get through to me.*

*Easy, eh?*

*So, grab a phone as soon as you can. I'm yearning to put an end to your None-Too-Happiness.*

ZinderZunder

*PS Don't forget – say it with every bit of passion in your heart. Otherwise it won't work.*

## 17:01

It's a joke! A trick! One of those TV shows where they play games on people. Perhaps I'm being filmed right now! They're waiting for me to rush to a phone and make a fool of myself.

And yet . . .

The way the letter followed me – that didn't look like a trick! And the way it jumped in and out of the water . . . If it's a trick, how did they do it? There's no strings! No magnets! No remote control –

Gee whiz! The letter's flown out of my hand! It's hovering in front of me! This *can't* be a trick!

Now it's wriggling a corner.

As if it's . . . waving goodbye!

I wave back.

Weeeshhh!

The letter's flown away! Right up to the sky. So fast, I can't even see it any more. And there's not a breeze in the air!

This is for *real*! That means . . .

Quick! A phone!

## 17:11

Here's one! A public phone box on the Square. I'll use this. Can't phone from home after all. Not with everyone listening –

No! It's broken!

What now? The Trillian Geezers! No, they haven't got a phone! What am I going to do? There's no more public phones!

Got no choice.

I'll have to go home –

## 17:17

Dear One-Time Little Gentleman

We've all gone to the pub to celebrate Baby Fleur's first steps. (Of course, I'm only going to have a lemonade.) We waited and waited for you, but, as I said to everyone, you've probably gone to the Trillian Geezers in a sulk and won't be back for hours.

However, if you get back early and want to join us, make sure you wear proper clothes and shoes. If you don't want to join us the front-door key's under the doormat.

See you later
Mumzie
xxx

**17:19**

What luck! Everyone'll be out for ages . . .
Where's the key? Ah! Here!

**17:23**

I'm sitting on the stairs. Phone
in my lap. My heart's beating
very fast.
    Pick up the receiver.
    Buzzzzz.
    Take a deep breath.
    Then –
    'ZinderZunder!'

**17:24**

Buzzzzz.
    Nothing.
    Put the receiver back.
    Couldn't have said it right. Not with – oh, what
was it again? Every bit of passion in my heart. Try
again!
    Pick up receiver.
    Buzzzzz.
    Deep breath.
    'ZINDERZUNDER!'
    Buzzzzz.
    Still nothing!

**17:29**

Gee whiz! I could have sworn I said it with total
heartfelt passion! But . . . obviously not! Got to
keep trying.
    Lift receiver.

Buzzzzz.
'ZinderZunDER!'
Buzzzzz.
Again –
'ZinderZUNder!'
Buzzzzz.

**17:31**
'Zinnnda-
Zunnnda!'
　Buzzzzz.

**18:03**
'ZinderrrZunderrr!'

**18:45**
'ZinDERzunDER!'

**19:42**
'ZiiiiinnnderZuuuuunnnder!'

**20:01**
'ZzzzzinderZzzzzunder!'

**20:33**
'ZINDERZUND –'

**20:34**
What's that? Footsteps! Oh no! No! Mumzie and Daddy Rosco are coming home! Look! It's dark outside! I've been saying 'ZinderZunder' for hours and hours! My throat's so sore –

'ZinderZu –'

'WAAARGH!'

No! Now Baby Fleur's crying! Must be past her bedtime!

I've got to say it! Now! Can't wait! Now!

Footsteps closer.

'ZinderZunder!'

Voices.

'Oh, ZinderZunder!'

Click!

Ring!

'Hello, ZinderZunder speaking!'

**20:35**
Did it! And listen to that voice! So deep and distorted. Like it's bubbling up through an ocean.

'Oh . . . a razzmatazz good evening to you Mr . . . er . . . ZinderZunder. My name's –'

'You're Max Huckabee.'

'Gee whiz! How did you know that?'

'I've got a magic phone, dingbat. It tells me who you are and where you live. 14 Paradise Square. Just you and your mother, Margo. Correct?'

'Almost! But it's not just me and Mumzie any more. There's Daddy Rosco.'

'Rosco! Let's check my records here . . . Do you mean Rosco Blossom? He's supposed to be living at 23 Paradise Square with his mum, known as Granny Blossom.'

'Well, he's here now. Has been for about a year. Oh no!'

'What's wrong, Max?'

'Mumzie! Rosco! And Baby Fleur! They're almost at the front door. Oh, gee whiz! Can you phone me back tomorrow?'

' 'Fraid not! You only get one chance! It's now or never!'

**20:36**

'I-I-I can't think. Mumzie and Daddy Rosco are right outside now –'

'And, Max, just one more thing: You have to tell me what you want in five words exactly.'

'WHAAATT?!'

'Five words! Not one word less. Or one word more.'

'But . . . that's stupid!'

'Listen, I don't make up the rules. This is magic. And unless you do it in five words, it just won't work. *Comprendez?*'

**20:37**

Mumzie's looking for her key.

'WAAARGHHH!'

'Oh, gee whiz . . . What I want is for Mumzie –'

'More than five words already!'

'What? Oh, geee whizzz!'

Still looking for key.

'WAAARGHHH!'

'THERE, THERE, BOOTIFUL!'

'Gee whiz! Think! Think clearly . . . What I want is for –'

'Already five!'

'But I need more words!'

'Look, Max – don't say "What I want". Just jump straight in with it. Try again!'

Mumzie's found her key.

'MUMZIE AND . . . WELL, MOST PEOPLE I KNOW SHOULD –'

'Too many words!'

The key's in the lock –

## 20:38

'Geee whizzz!'

'Try again, Max.'

'I can't do it!'

'Try!'

The key is turning.

'EVERYONE MUST – Oh, I can't think.'

'Do it, Max!'

Opening.

'EVERYONE MUST DIG MY RAZZMATAZZ!'

'Thank you for your request, Max Huckabee. It will be granted. Please wait for magic.'

Click.

Buzzzzz.

## 20:39

'Darling! There you are! You missed such a wonderful evening. Fancy storming off like that!

Mumzie's feeling in such a good mood now. I'm sure somebody must have slipped something naughty in my lemonade. I do declare your Mumzie's head is giddier than a litter of tipsy kittens in a tumble dryer set to Fastest Spin Ever – lordy-lordy, what are you doing with the phone on your lap?'

'Gee whiz – nothing, Mumzie.'

## 00:00

'Midnight,' sighs Max, sitting up in bed, 'and still no magic.'

All evening long he'd been waiting for something to happen. He'd helped Mumzie wash up the party dishes, watching her closely for some change, some sign, some . . . anything! At one point she had said, 'Lordy-lordy, darling! Stop staring at me like that! I do declare you're studying me harder than a biologist in a Spot the Germ competition.'

And later, as they all sat watching the TV, Daddy Rosco had suddenly jumped to his feet and cried, 'TURN THE TELLY DOWN!' And Max thought, This is it! The magic has started! But Daddy Rosco thought he'd heard Baby Fleur crying upstairs. That's all.

No magic.

And now, as Max waits, bathed in moonlight, listening to Daddy Rosco's snoring in the next room, he's beginning to wonder if the magic will ever come.

Perhaps ZinderZunder can't do it! Perhaps my wish was too big! Even for someone like him –

Wait! What's that? Oh, it's only a car backfiring!
No magic, no magic!

## 00:12

Max lies down in bed and pulls the blanket up to
his chin.

Might as well forget all about it! Too tired to
stay awake anyway – Wait. What's that? Oh, it's
only milk bottles being knocked over. A cat,
probably. No magic, no magic –

Rap!

What's that?

Rap! Rap!

Something at the window!

Max jumps out of bed and sees –

## 00:14

A bird! Gee whiz! I've never seen a bird like this!
Looks like a bright-blue kingfisher. But it's got the
tail feathers of a peacock. And feathers on its head
like a cockatoo –

Rap! Rap! Rap!

Its beak's hitting the glass! Wants to come in!
This must be it!

Max flings open the window –

Flap! Flap!

The bird flies round the room a few times.

Then comes to rest on Max's bed.

## 00:17

Max stares down at the bird, waiting.

The bird stares up at Max, waiting.

'Wh-what?' wonders Max. 'What am I

supposed to –'

Gee whiz! There's something in your beak! Let me see . . . It's like a small stone! No! It's a seed, I think. The size of a large chestnut. Except it's yellow –

'Wait! Don't go!'

But the bird flies out of the window and disappears into the night . . .

What am I supposed to do with this – Hang on! Something's written all round it! Let's see! Gee whiz – the writing's so small. Can hardly see it. Turn my bedside lamp on.

There! That's better. I can just about make out . . .

## 00:19

INSTRUCTIONS

1) PLANT ME IN MOONLIGHT.
2) PLANT ME THE DEPTH OF YOUR LITTLE FINGER.
3) PICK UP THE FIRST BOOK YOU SEE.
4) THROW BOOK IN AIR SO THAT IT LANDS FACE DOWN AND OPEN.
5) TURN BOOK OVER AND LOOK AT THE NUMBER OF THE RIGHT-HAND PAGE.
6) WHISPER YOUR FIVE-WORD WISH TO ME THIS NUMBER OF TIMES. THE WHISPERING MUST BE VERY FAST AND WITHOUT A BREAK.
7) PLEASE WAIT FOR MAGIC.

## 00:21

I'm creeping down the stairs! Gee whiz! Have to be quiet! That's it! One more step!

Now out into –

## 00:24

– the garden! Glad the back door opened without creaking! And I'm glad I've put my new tap-dancing shoes on. Should have put some socks on though. They're rubbing my heels a little bit. Still – at least I can walk across the rubble without hurting my feet.

Now . . . where's a patch of moonlight?

There! Right at the back!

## 00:27

I'm digging a hole! Ouch! Little sharp stones are

grazing my fingers. Should have worn gloves. No time now! Gotta keep digging! Is it as deep as my little finger? Check . . .

Mmm . . . Not quite yet.

Dig some more!

Try it now!

That's it!

Drop the seed in the hole!

Put the earth back on top!

Pat it flat.

Now what?

Oh – yes – the book!

## 00:30

I'm in the kitchen!

A book . . .

Where? Where? Ah!

There's one!

What is it? A cook book – well, it would be, I suppose.

Won't throw the book in the air here. Don't want to wake anyone. Back out into the –

## 00:31

– garden. And . . .

Throw!

Ka-flop!

Turn book.

Look at right-hand page.

19.

Gee whiz! I've got to whisper my five-word wish nineteen times!

Oh well, best get started!

Kneel on the ground.

Lean forward.

Mouth almost touching the rubble where it's planted . . .

**00:33**

'Everyone must dig my razzmatazz! Everyone must dig my razzmatazz! Everyone must dig my razzmatazz! Everyone must dig my razzmatazz! Everyone must dig my razzmatazz! Everyone must dig my razzmatazz! Everyone must dig my razzmatazz! Everyone must dig my razzmatazz! Everyone must dig my razzmatazz! Everyone must dig my –'

**00:34**

'WAAAAARGHHHHH!'

No! I was almost there! Quick – gotta hide! Mumzie will get up in a –

There! Her bedroom light's come on.

Tuck myself in the corner.

'WAAAAARGHHHHH!'

Hope Mumzie doesn't look in my room! If she sees I'm not there – Oh, try not to think about it!

Just hide.

And wait . . .

**00:37**

Baby Fleur's stopped crying.

Mumzie's gone back to bed. Her light's gone out.

The garden's still again.

Just moonlight.

And insects.
And me – kneeling
on the ground and –

**00:39**

'Everyonemustdigmyrazzmatazzeveryonemustdi
gmyrazzmatazzeveryonemustdigmyrazzmatazze
veryonemustdigmyrazzmatazzeveryonemustdig
myrazzmatazzeveryonemustdigmyrazzmatazzev
eryonemustdigmyrazzmatazzeveryonemustdigm
yrazzmatazzeveryonemustdigmyrazzmatazzever
yonemustdigmyrazzmatazzeveryonemustdigmyr
azzmatazzeveryonemustdigmyrazzmatazzeveryo
nemustdigmyrazzmatazzeveryonemustdigmyraz
zmatazzeveryonemustdigmyrazzmatazzeveryone
mustdigmyrazzmatazzeveryonemustdigmyrazzm
atazzeveryonemustdigmyrazzmatazzeveyonemus
tdigmyrazzmatazz.'

**00:41**

Phew!
That's it! I've done everything.
Now what?
Well . . . just wait, I suppose . . .

**00:50**

Nothing's happened yet.

**00:59**

Garden's very still.
Still waiting.

**01:10**

I'm getting cold now. Shivering. Should pop
upstairs for a blanket. But I don't want to miss
anything.
At the moment though . . . nothing.

**01:22**

Still nothing.

**01:33**

Nothing!

**01:37**

Perhaps it's not going to happen tonight! I know
the instructions said PLEASE WAIT FOR MAGIC,
but they didn't say exactly *how* long to wait.
It might be days.
Weeks!
Years!
Oh, I'm getting so tired! And cold! And sitting

on this slab of concrete has made my bum go
numb –

**01:39**
A noise!
   What –
   Look!
   There!
   Where I planted the seed . . .
   Geeeee whiiiiizzzzz!
   A green shoot!

**01:40**
It's growing! So fast! Like those fast-motion films
where a whole lifetime of a plant is squeezed into
a few seconds –
   Bigger!
   Bigger!!
   The green shoot sprouts branches.
   The branches sprout leaves.
   Bigger!!!
   Bigger!!!!
   Bigger!!!!!
   It's becoming a tree!

**01:41**
Up!
   Up!
   Up!
   Branches just above my head now!
   The tree is twisting and turning. The bark is
gnarled. The leaves are –
   The leaves are the brightest blue I've ever seen.

Quite beautiful!

## 01:43

It's stopped growing!
  About three times taller than me.
  And look!
  There's buds on the branches.
  Flower buds.
  As big as my fist and covered with pink hairs.
  So . . . what now?
  How's this going to make my wish come true?
  I don't get it –

## 01:44

'WHAT'S GOING ON, SHORT STUFF?'

'Daddy Rosco! Gee whiz! What are you doing up?'

'I'M GOING TO WORK, SHORT STUFF. TWELVE-HOUR SHIFT, DON'T FORGET! TWO IN THE MORNING TO TWO IN THE AFTERNOON – BLOW ME! WHAT'S THAT?'

Daddy Rosco's eyes have just got used to the dark now. He's seen the tree for the first time.

Eyes wide – and wearing only his boxer shorts and slippers – he walks the length of the garden and looks up at the –

'IT'S A TREE, SHORT STUFF!'

'Indeedy, yes, Daddy Rosco.'

'BUT . . . WHERE? . . . HOW –'

And then –

One of the fist-sized flower buds opens.

Qwisssss!

## 01:47

Beautiful multicoloured petals unfold.

With bright-yellow tendrils inside.

Gee whiz! Look at that! It's like a giant orchid or something! And the smell! Like . . . like the sweetest chocolate –

'BOOTIFUL!'

Daddy Rosco has smelt the flower. He moves closer. Buries his face amongst the petals. Sniffs again. 'BOOTIFUL! BOOTIFUL!'

And then –

'SHORT STUFF!' gasps Daddy Rosco, suddenly staring at Max. 'DANCE FOR ME!'

## 01:48

'Wh-what, Daddy Rosco?'

'YOUR DANCING'S THE MOST BOOTIFUL THING IN THE WORLD! OH, WHY DIDN'T I EVER REALIZE IT BEFORE? I'VE BEEN SO STUPID! YOUR DANCING IS MORE BOOTIFUL THAN ALL THE SHINIEST CHROME ON THE SHINIEST CARS! OH, SHORT STUFF, I'D GIVE ALL THE MUSCLES IN MY THIGHS TO SEE YOU DANCE RIGHT NOW!'

'Well, thank you, Daddy Rosco! I'd really love to. Tell you what, tomorrow I'll –'

'TOMORROW?' shrieks Daddy Rosco. 'I CAN'T WAIT THAT LONG, SHORT STUFF! I WANT TO SEE IT NOW! YOU HEAR ME? NOW! NOW! NOW!'

## 01:50

Look at Daddy Rosco. He's almost begging. His eyes are pleading. Oh well, it's what I wanted so –

Tap!

Tap!

Tippity –

'BOOTIFUL! OH, MY SKIN IS TINGLING ALL OVER! BLOOD RUSHING LIKE I'VE LIFTED

THE HEAVIEST OF WEIGHTS! BOOTIFUL!
BOOTIFUL –'

**01:53**

'Lordy-lordy! What's going on out here?' Mumzie
strides out into the garden, wrapping her frilly
pink dressing gown around her. 'I do declare
you're making more noise than a town crier in a
Who Can Make The Loudest Cry At Night And
Disturb All The Neighbours competition! Daddy
Rosco – have you been drinking again?'

'DRINKING? CERTAINLY NOT, PRETTY
LADY! PLEASE DO NOT DISTRESS YOURSELF.'

'How can I help it? You out in the middle of the
night! Half naked! And honestly, Max, I thought
you'd know better. In your pyjamas! You'll catch a
terrible chill – Argh! Wh-where did that tree come
from? Darling? Daddy Rosco? Tell me –'

And, as Mumzie speaks –

Qwisssss!

'– Mmmmm, that smell! Chocolate!' And then,
her eyes wide, Mumzie looks at Max and cries,
'Dance, darling! Dance for Mumzie now!'

**01:55**

'But, Mumzie, it's the middle of the night!'

'So?'

'And the neighbours –'

'Oh, who cares about the neighbours, darling?
Honestly! What do neighbours matter in the light
of your tapping genius? If they don't appreciate it,
they're fools! Like I was a fool! Dance, darling!
Dance! Dance! Dance!'

**01:58**

Look at Mumzie! She's begging for me to dance
too. Her eyes are pleading. Oh well, it's what I
wanted –

'Just a few quick steps, Mumzie.'

'Thank you, darling!'

'THANK YOU, SHORT STUFF.'

Tap!

Tap!

Tap!

Tippity! Tippity –

'Oh, darling! I do declare listening to you makes
me feel as excited as a zillion dog tails in a Tail
Wagging competition!'

**02:01**

'WAAAAARGHHHHH!'

'I've woken Baby Fleur –'

'Ignore her, darling!'

'IGNORE HER, SHORT-STUFF!'

'Ig-*ignore* her?' Max stops dancing. 'But – gee
whiz! – Mumzie! Daddy Rosco! She might need
something! Listen to her!'

'WAAARGHHH!'

'Honestly, darling! All she needs is a kiss and
cuddle! But there's not time for that! Lordy-lordy,
Mumzie can't waste time kissing and cuddling
that gurgling, talentless idiot when I can watch –
Oh, darling! Mumzie can't wait another moment!
Dance! DANCE! DANCE!'

**02:10**

Look at them! Their eyes are glaring with

desperation! They're trembling! I'll give them just
a little bit more –

Tap!

Tap!

Tippity! Click! Spin!

Tap!

Tap!

Tippity! Spin! Click –

## 02:14

'What's going on down there?'

'What's all the racket?'

'Keep it quiet!'

'People trying to sleep!'

'Work in the morning!'

Bedroom lights are being turned on!

Neighbours, groggy and in their nightclothes, are calling out and –

Qwisssssssssss!

Another bud opens.

Qwisssssssssssss!
Another.
Qwisssssssssssss!
Qwisssssssssssss!
Qwisssssssssssss!
Every flower on the tree is opening up!
The smell of chocolate is overpowering.
And now –
A gentle breeze . . .

## 02:17
'Who wants to sleep? – DANCE!'
    'Forget about work! – DANCE!'
    'Forget about everything! – DANCE!'
    Look at them all! Watching from their windows.
And look! There! Even stray cats are coming to
watch.
    Gee whiz! I've got no choice.
    Tap!
    Tap!
    Tippity! Click! Click –

## 02:21
Ouch – I'm getting a blister! Can't dance for much
more . . .
    'Gee whiz, everyone! I'm so glad you dig my
razzmatazzing. But . . . well, you can all go back to
bed now! I've got a blister and –'
    'Honestly, darling! Don't make a fuss!'
    'WHAT DOES A BLISTER MATTER, SHORT
STUFF?'
    And all the neighbours yell, 'DANCE!'
    'But my blister is so painful I can't –'

All the neighbours are climbing out of their windows now.

And storming through their back doors.

Clambering over fences.

They're angry with me!

And everyone's chanting, 'DANCE! DANCE! DANCE!'

**02:24**

CRASHHH!

Someone's fence has been knocked down.

CRUUUNNNCH!

And they're walking over rose bushes!

SQUISHHH!

And flowers!

SMASH!

A milk bottle is knocked over.

'DANCE! DANCE! DANCE!'

They're getting closer and closer . . .

**02:26**

Now Mumzie is looking at me. Gee whiz! Not just looking! *Glaring!* Like there's something crazy inside her.

'There, darling! You see what you've done? You're turning your fans frantic! You see, we don't just *love* your dancing! We don't just *want* it! We *need* it, darling! AND WE NEED IT NOWWW!'

**02:27**

Gee whiz! No choice!

Tap!

Tap! Tap!

Tap! Click! Spin!
Tap! Tippity –

**02:31**
Look! They've all quietened down. Watching me with rapt attention. I'm their idol. Their hero.

Mumzie's weeping with joy.

Gee whiz! – So is Daddy Rosco!

They've got their arms round each other.

Even some of the neighbours look close to tears.

Tap!

Tap!

Tap!

Tippity!

Tippity!

Spin! Click! Tap –

Ouch! I'm getting a blister on the other foot now. Got to stop for a second –

'No! Darling! Dance!'

'DANCE, SHORT STUFF!'

'DANCE! DANCE! DANCE!'

There's something scary in all their eyes.

No choice but to –

**02:37**
Tap!

Tap!

Tap!

Tap!

Legs getting tired now. Wobbly. Feet sore –

'WAAARGHHH!'

And Baby Fleur still crying. No one's taking any

notice of her. Look! Mumzie's acting like she can't even hear her –

'WAAARGHHH!'

I hope Baby Fleur's all right. Anything could have happened. Perhaps she's hungry. Or thirsty! Scared! – Of course! She *must* be scared! All this noise outside. And no one coming to comfort her. She needs a kiss and a cuddle. And if no one else is going to do it, then I'll have to –

## 02:41

'Darling! Where you going? Come back here! DANCE!'

'But I can't, Mumzie. Not with Baby Fleur –'

'Forget Baby Fleur!'

'But . . . I CAN'T, MUMZIE! I CAN'T!'

Quick! Make a dash for it!

Into the house!
That's it!
Slam the back door behind me.

**02:42**
THRACK!
Lock it!
And now –
Up the stairs!
Listen to Mumzie. And Daddy Rosco. And all the neighbours!
They're howling for me! Kicking at the door!
'WAAARGH!'
'Don't be scared, Baby Fleur! Brother Max is coming!'
Gee whiz! Guess that's what she *will* call me. After all, I *am* her brother. Never thought of myself like that before –

**02:43**
Into Baby Fleur's room!
There's her little cot!
Oh, look at her!
She's been crying so much her face is wet with tears.
Pick her up –
'Hush, Baby Fleur. Hush now! It's all right.'
Gee whiz! She's stopped crying!
And look –
She's smiling at me! What a pretty smile. Never noticed before. And what sparkling eyes –

**02:44**

CRASH!

SMASH!

The back door's been broken down! And windows are smashing!

They're in the house!

'DARLING – DANCE!'

'SHORT STUFF – DANCE!'

'DANCE! DANCE! DANCE!'

'WAAARGH!'

'Shush, Baby Fleur. Don't worry – don't let them scare you.'

'DANCE!'

'DANCE!'

'DANCE! DANCE! DANCE!'

Listen to them! Gee whiz! They're right outside the door now –

It's swung open.

There's Mumzie!

Everyone else behind her.

She's like a maniac general in charge of a maniac army.

'DARLING! DANCE! NOW!'

**02:49**

They're all pushing their way into the room.

Climbing over each other almost.

And treading on things.

Breaking toys!

Shattering dolls.

'Stop! You're going to hurt Baby Fleur if you're not careful –'

'DARLING – DANCE!'

'SHORT STUFF – DANCE!'
'DANCE! DANCE! DANCE!'
More and more people
squeezing into the room.

I'm trapped! No way out!
Help!

**02:53**
Wait! The window! It's open!
If I can just climb out. There's
a big ledge that runs along the
back of the house. I can walk
along that and –

'DARLING – DANCE!'
'SHORT STUFF! –
DANCE!'
'DANCE!
DANCE!
DANCE!'

Hurry!
Pick up Baby Fleur!
Then . . . with one hand –
Open window!
There!
Now . . . lift my leg up!
Sitting on window ledge now.
Nearly out –
'DON'T, DARLING!' Mumzie's grabbed hold of
my leg. 'YOU'VE GOT TO DANCE!'
'Let me go, Mumzie! You'll hurt Baby Fleur!'
I'm kicking to get free . . .
There! Done it!
Now – quick! Other leg out! And . . .

Walk along this ledge . . .

**02:59**
Keep a firm grip on Baby Fleur. Look at her! She's stopped crying now. Looking at me with such trust –

Gee whiz! I've come to the end of the ledge! Where to now –

'DARLING!'

'SHORT STUFF!'

No! Mumzie and Daddy Rosco have followed me out on to the ledge.

Some of the neighbours too!

Others are rushing back into the house and out on to the street.

**03:01**
'DANCE! DANCE! DANCE!'

Sounds of things smashing and breaking everywhere.

Got to think! Quick!

There! A shed! I can easily jump down on to that! Gee whiz! It's like something out of an action film.

How's Baby Fleur?

She's fine! I've got her held quite safely.

Look! What luck! A ladder! Someone must have been cleaning their windows!

Now . . . just climb down . . .

Carefully . . .

Carefully . . .

Ground level!

I'm more of an acrobat than I thought.

Now . . . I've got to get to the Trillian Geezers as soon as possible. They'll help! If I cut down this side alley, I should end up on the Square and I can –

## 03:05

GEEEEEWHIIIIIZZZZZ!

People!

Hundreds of them!

Looks as if everyone in the Square is up. In their nightclothes. And looking for me!

Looking under cars.

Under bushes.

In dustbins.

All chanting, 'DANCE! DANCE! DANCE!'

Most of them have got torches!

Beams of light darting everywhere.

They haven't seen me yet.

If I'm quiet, I'll just slink along this wall and –

**03:06**

'Mercy! There you are, Little Huck!'

Granny Blossom! In her nightdress! Her face covered with moisturizing cream. And she's grabbing hold of my arm –

'Let me go, Granny Blossom!'

'Not till you dance, Little Huck! Mercy – how can you ever forgive me! The way I used to laugh! I didn't realize! I was a sinner! But now I've repented! Forgive me, Little Huck! Forgive and – DANCE! DANCE!'

'Keep your voice down, Granny Blossom! Please! The others will hear you –'

'But they *should* hear me! Look at them! They're as desperate as I am. Desperate for your razzmatazz! – LOOK, EVERYONE! I'VE GOT HIM! HE'S HERE! HEEERE!'

**03:07**

'DARLING!'

'SHORT STUFF!'

'DANCE! DANCE! DANCE!'

They're rushing this way!

Climbing over cars!

Trampling bushes!

Got to get away!

One quick tug while Granny Blossom's looking at the approaching crowd –

There!

'MERCY! WHERE YOU GOING, LITTLE –'

And run!

Run!

**03:10**

'Oh, it's all right, Baby Fleur . . . Don't panic . . .
We'll soon be with the Trillian Geezers . . . They'll
look after us . . . They'll know what to do . . . Oh,
gee whiz, the crowd's getting closer and closer . . .
Listen to them . . . You OK, Baby Fleur? Not
shaking you about too much, am I?'

'DARLING – DANCE!'

'SHORT STUFF – DANCE!'

'LITTLE HUCK – DANCE!'

'DANCE! DANCE! DANCE!'

'Oh, don't be scared, Baby Fleur –'

'Cooo-eee, Maxie!'

**03:13**

'Gee whiz! Aunt Kiki! Let me go!'

'Oh, Maxie! Luverducks! Who would have
thought it? Me, out in my night-blooming-clothes!
With my hair in curlers! But I had to, Maxie!
Because I need –'

'I know what you need, Aunt Kiki! But I can't!
My feet are covered in blisters!'

'I don't mind!'

'Well, *I* mind! They hurt! Let me go!'

The mob's getting closer and closer. Gotta get
away –

One tug.

There!

'MAXIE!'

Now run!

Run!

Run!

**03:15**

'DARLING – DANCE!'

'SHORT STUFF – DANCE!'

'LITTLE HUCK – DANCE!'

'MAXIE – DANCE!'

'DANCE! DANCE! DANCE!'

'It's all right, Baby Fleur! . . . Nothing will happen to you while I'm with you! Ah, look! Baby Fleur's smiling at me again . . . How beautiful she looks when she –'

**03:17**

'maXIE-weED!'

'Cousin Otis! Let me go –'

'CAN'T do THat! GOTta SEE YA DANCE! I'VE been SUCH a TOTal NERD! FORGive ME, MaXIE-WeED! you are More IMPressIVE THan ALL MUSCLES put TOgetHer! DANCE for ME, MAXIE-weed! DANce!'

Tug!

Free!

Run!

**03:20**

'DARLING – DANCE!'

'SHORT STUFF – DANCE!'

'LITTLE HUCK – DANCE!'

'MAXIE – DANCE!'

'MaxIE-weED – DAnce!'

'DANCE! DANCE! DANCE!'

Nearly there . . . Ouch, my blisters are really hurting . . . Hang in there, Baby Fleur! Ah! There's the Trillian Geezers' house – Quick! Quick! Ring the –

DA-DING! DA-DONG!

Gee whiz! They must still be asleep. They're such deep sleepers! And they couldn't have smelt the chocolate flowers yet –

DA-DING! DA-DONG!

DA-DING! DA-DONG!

DA-DING! DA-DONG!

'WAKE UP, BIG 'N' LITTLE TRILLS!'

**03:23**

The mob's getting closer.

And stomping over everything –

Smashhh!

Crashhh!

Traammpplle!

DA-DING –

'WAKE UP! WAKE UP!'

The bedroom light's come on!

And there –

It's Big 'n' Little Trills. In their nightshirts! Groggily wondering what's happening –

'WAIT! BIG TRILL! LITTLE TRILL! DON'T

OPEN THE WINDOW! NOT YET! YOU'VE GOT
TO BLOCK YOUR NOSES WITH SOMETHING
FIRST! I KNOW IT SOUNDS CRAZY! BUT
PLEASE! TRUST ME! YOU MUSTN'T SMELL
ANYTHING! PLEASE! THEN LET ME IN! AND
HURRY! HURRY!'

**03:24**
SMASHHH!
　CRASHHH!
　TRAAMMPPLLE!
　'HURRY, BIG 'N' LITTLE TRILLS! THEY'RE
GETTING CLOSER!'
　'DARLING – DANCE!'
　'SHORT STUFF – DANCE!'
　'LITTLE HUCK – DANCE!'
　'MAXIE – DANCE!'
　'MAXie-weED – danCE!'
　'DANCE!　DANCE!　DANCE!　DANCE!
DANCE!'
　The front door's opening –
　'Quick! Let me in! Ah – you've put pegs on your
noses! Razzmatazz idea! You can't smell anything,
can you?'
　'Indeedy, no, WonderMax. But the pegs are
rather painful. Right, Brother Little Trill?'
　'Indeedy, yes, Brother Big Trill. And make our
voices sound funny –'
　'Forget the pain and funny voices! It's nothing
compared to –'
　SMASH!
　CRASH!
　TRAMPLE!

'Quick! Shut the door! Lock it! Bolt it!'

Slam!

Lock!

Bolt!

'Heavens to Betsy! What's going on WonderMax?'

'Good golly Miss Molly! Has the whole world gone crazy, WonderMax?'

'Indeedy, yes, Big 'n' Little Trills. That's just it,

THE WHOLE WORLD'S GONE CRAZY –'
THOOM!
'Gee whiz! They're breaking the door down!'

## 03:26

'Heavens to Betsy!'
'Good golly Miss Molly!'
THOOOM!
'You've got to help me, Big 'n' Little Trills. Full explanations later! If they get me, they'll just make me –'
'DANCE! DANCE! DANCE!'
'You hear that, Big 'n' Little Trills! And my feet hurt! And . . . I'm tired . . . And I'm afraid for poor Baby Fleur here –'
THOOOOM!
CRAAACK!
'GEEE WHIIIZZZ! – THE DOOR'S SPLITTING OPEN!'

## 03:28

'WonderMax – in the living room! Quick! Heavens to Betsy! Shut the living-room door, Brother Little Trill!'
'Good golly Miss Molly, yes, Brother Big Trill!'
SLAM!
'Put the table up against it, Big 'n' Little Trills!'
'Indeedy, yes, WonderMax! Help me, Brother Little Trill!'
Push!
Puuushhh!
'There, WonderMax! The table should keep them out –'

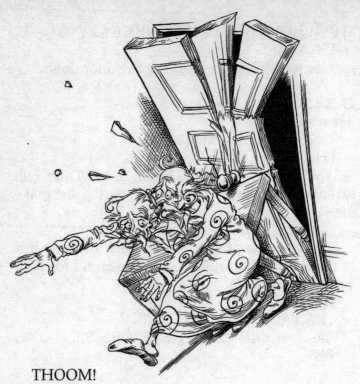

THOOM!

'Heavens to Betsy! Now they're knocking *this* door down too!'

'Good golly Miss Molly! They're not going to give up!'

THOOOM!

THOOOOM!

CRAAAAACK!

'GEE WHIZ! THE DOOR'S GIVING WAY! NOOOOO!'

**03:30**

Look at Mumzie! Clambering her way through the shattered door! Her hair's full of petals and twigs!

Her fingernails are broken! She's grazed all over!
Eyes wide! Mouth salivating! I've never seen her
this way. She's like a wild animal!

So is Daddy Rosco.

And Granny Blossom.

And Aunt Kiki.

And Cousin Otis.

And all the neighbours!

Everyone's squeezing into the room behind
Mumzie.

Knocking furniture over!

Breaking things!

Trampling!

**03:32**

'Heavens to Betsy!' cries Big Trill. 'How dare you
come in without even knocking! I've never seen
such truly ungracious behaviour – Oh, please be
careful of that vase! It was a present from –'

Smash!

'Good golly Miss Molly!' cries Little Trill. 'How
dare you come in without being invited! Oh,
please be careful with that newspaper cutting –'

Rip!

**03:33**

'WonderMax! Get behind me! Quickly! Brother
Little Trill, you stand beside me so we're double
protection for our precious fellow! I don't think
I've ever seen such a hostile audience.'

'I agree, Brother Big Trill! It's even more hostile
than the drunken hen-party we were mistakenly
booked to entertain at. Remember?'

'I'll never forget it, Brother Little Trill. Someone threw a pair of knickers at me and told me to get my thermal underpants off! Quite horrific!'

'But Big 'n' Little Trills – Mumzie and everyone aren't being hostile! At least, not in the same way! They're like this because they *want* me to perform! Listen!'

'DANCE! DANCE! DANCE!'

'Heavens to Betsy, WonderMax! I've never seen the like! Now . . . you keep hold of Baby Fleur. And stay behind me and Brother Little Trill. I've managed audiences of all complexions – Let me talk to them.'

And with that, Big Trill spreads his arms and, smiling as wide as possible, steps forward and announces –

**03:35**
'Welcome, ladies and gentlemen! Uninvited though you are, welcome!'

For a moment, Big Trill's voice startles the rampant horde to silence.

'Naturally, Brother Little Trill and I are thrilled – nay, overwhelmed – that you admire our precious WonderMax's dancing so much that you see fit to demolish half the Square and our house! After all, it was us – the Trillian Geezers the Walloping Caesars – who taught him all he knows. But, ladies and gentlemen, please, I beg you to consider that this is neither the time nor the place –'

'SHUT IT, YOU BORING OLD FART!' yells Mumzie.

'Mumzie!' gasps Max.

'Heavens to Betsy! I never thought I'd hear such ungenteel language from –'

'TO HELL WITH BEING GENTEEL!' shrieks Mumzie. 'I'M FED UP WITH ALWAYS HAVING TO THINK TWICE ABOUT WHAT I SAY AND HOW I LOOK! ALWAYS WORRIED ABOUT WHAT THE NEIGHBOURS THINK OF ME! HAVING THEM LOOK DOWN THEIR NOSES AT ME BECAUSE I'VE GOT NO CARPETS AND NO FLOWERS IN MY GARDEN! WELL, THEY'RE NOT LOOKING DOWN THEIR NOSES NOW! I'VE GOT SOMETHING THEY'LL NEVER HAVE! I'VE GOT A GENIUS FOR A SON! SO I DON'T CARE WHAT PEOPLE THINK OF ME ANY MORE! YOU HEAR ME? ALL I CARE ABOUT IS . . . OH, DANCE, DARLING! DANCE! DANCE!'

'SHORT STUFF – DANCE!'
'LITTLE HUCK – DANCE!'
'MAXIE – DANCE!'
'maxIE-Weed – danCE!'
'DANCE! DANCE! DANCE!'

**03:38**

Gee whiz! They're moving closer!

'Heavens to Betsy! I don't like the look of this one little bit! Listen to me, WonderMax and Brother Little Trill! On the count of three – I want us all to run out the back door! And, WonderMax – make sure you keep a firm grip on Baby Fleur. Understood?'

'Indeedy, yes, Big Trill.'

'Good golly Miss Molly, yes, Brother Big Trill.'

Closer . . .
Another vase falls.
Smash!
'One . . .'
Another.
Smash!
'Two . . .'
Closer.
Smash!
Smash!
'THREEEEE!'

**03:41**
Gee whiz! Made it!

Out through the back door!

But listen to them behind us! Howling and screaming and –

'WAAARGHHH!'

'Oh, there, there, don't cry . . . I know it's scary . . . But I'm here to protect you. Honest! Nothing will happen to you while your Brother Max is with you –'

'Down this alley, WonderMax!'

'Indeedy, yes, Big Trill!'

'Now into this house, WonderMax!'

'Indeedy, yes, Big Trill!'

The back door's been left open! Quick! Shut the door behind me! Lock it!

There!

'Heavens to Betsy! Look at the state of this kitchen! The mob have already been through here by the looks of it!'

'No, Big Trill, that's . . . that's not it! We're in my Aunt Kiki's house! It always looks like this –'

'DANCE! DANCE! DANCE!'

'They're outside, Big 'n' Little Trills!'

'Lock the windows, Brother Little Trill!'

'Good golly Miss Molly, yes, Brother Big Trill!'

'We've got to think of a plan, WonderMax. Quickly! There must be something we can do! Anything! Think! How did it all start? Think!'

## 03:47

Smash!

'Gee whiz! They're breaking the windows –'

'WAAARGH!'

'Shush, Baby Fleur! Your Brother Max is here – I can't let anything happen to Baby Fleur! Look at the way she's holding on to me! She trusts me! She needs me –'

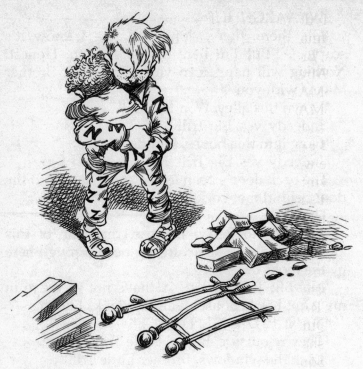

Smash!

Smash!

'HEAVENS TO BETSY!'

'GOOD GOLLY MISS MOLLY!'

'Gee whiz! Before long the whole city will smell the – Wait! That's it! Chocolate!'

'Oh really, WonderMax, this is no time to be thinking of your stomach!'

'No, no, Big Trill! It's not that! Listen! There's a tree in my garden. With flowers! The flowers smell of chocolate! We've got to get rid of it somehow – oh, don't ask me to explain. We've just got to chop the tree down – get rid of the smell! That's it!'

'I don't happen to have a chainsaw in my pyjamas at the moment, WonderMax. What about you, Brother Little Trill?'

'Afraid not, Brother Big Trill.'

SMAAASHHH!

SMAAASHHH!

**03:49**

'Gee whiz! We've got to do something! If not chop down the tree then . . . then . . . pick the flowers! That's it! We'll pick the flowers and get rid of them somehow –'

THOOM!

'They're knocking down the door again! There's just no stopping them. They're like . . . a plague of locusts or something –'

CRAAAAACK!

'Quick, Big 'n' Little Trills! Down the corridor. Shush, Baby Fleur . . . Now, I'll just peek out into the Square . . . All clear. Ready?'

'Ready, WonderMax.'

'Ready, WonderMax.'

'Then . . . RUUUNNN!'

**03:53**

Look at the state of the Square.

Like a tornado's been through it.

CRASH!

SMASH!

TRAMPLE!

Listen to them! Searching Aunt Kiki's house. They think we're still hiding in there. Well, that's just fine. Gives us more time!

'Be careful there, Big 'n' Little Trills. There's broken glass everywhere.'

'Don't you worry about us, my precious fellow. Let's just get to your house and put an end to this hullabaloo –'

'WHERE ARE YOU, DARLING?'

'WHERE YOU GOT TO, SHORT STUFF?'

'MERCY! WHERE ARE YOU, LITTLE HUCK?'

'SHOW YOUR BLOOMING SELF, MAXIE!'

'COme ouT WHerever yOU Are, maxIE-WEed!'

'Heavens to Betsy, WonderMax! It sounds like they're taking Aunt Kiki's house apart. A brick at a time. The Square's going to look like a war-zone by morning –'

**04:01**

'We're here, Big 'n' Little Trills! My house. Inside! Quick . . . That's it . . . Careful! There's some broken crockery there! Now – out into the garden – Oh, gee whiz! The smell of chocolate takes my breath away!'

'What a razzmatazz tree, WonderMax!'

'And such razzmatazz flowers –'

'Well, it's the flowers we've got to pick! And quick! Now . . . I'll just put Baby Fleur down here . . . at the base of the tree . . . There's not too much rubble here so she should be quite safe –'

'DARLING!'

'Listen! Mumzie's voice is getting louder! She must be out of Aunt Kiki's house now! We haven't much time! Big Trill – start picking the flowers! Little Trill – see that empty dustbin in the corner? Bring it over here! I'll start picking too! I'll climb up to get the flowers on the top branches. It's not too far – That's it, Little Trill! Put the dustbin there! Next to Baby Fleur. Now, as we pick the flowers – throw them in the bin!'

'But they'll still smell, WonderMax!'

'Good golly Miss Molly, yes, WonderMax.'

'Not if we slam the lid on top of them! And, well, even if we don't get rid of the smell completely, we might lessen the stink enough to talk some sense into them – Gee whiz! That gives me another idea! There's an air-freshener spray in the kitchen. That might help mask the flower smell! Can you get it, please, Little Trill?'

'At once, WonderMax!'

'Then, when you've done that, help us pick! Cos that's what we've got to do! Pick! Pick like we've never picked before!'

## 04:05

Max is picking.

Big Trill is picking.

Little Trill is picking.

And throwing the picked flowers into the dustbin!

'Gee whiz! Listen! They're getting closer –'

'DARLING!'

'SHORT STUFF!'

'LITTLE HUCK!'

'MAXIE!'

'MAxie-WeeD!'

'– and closer! They're searching the houses one by one! Pick, quick, Big 'n' Little Trills! Pick quick! Pick quick! Pick quick!'

**04:07**

'Pick quick, WonderMax!'

'Pick quick, WonderMax!'

Pick!

Pick!

SMASH!

CRASH!

TRAMPLE!

'Oh, gee whiz! Listen to that! Sounds like they're next door! We haven't much time! Now . . . I can just reach the top branches if I stand on this branch.'

'Be careful, WonderMax.'

'Don't worry about me, Big Trill. Just keep pick –'

'THERE YOU ARE, DARLING!'

**04:09**

'Mumzie's seen me! From next door's bedroom window! They'll be here any second, Big 'n' Little Trills! Pick quick! Pick quick!'

'We'll never make it, WonderMax!'

'Don't talk like that, Little Trill. Just be ready with the air freshener. And keep picking! Gee whiz! If there's ever a Pick An Exotic Flower And Throw It Into A Dustbin competition, we'll win hands down –'

'DARLING – DANCE!'

'WonderMax – they're here!'

'WonderMax – they're surrounding us!'

**04:11**

'Little Trill – you hold them off with the air

freshener. And get ready to slam the lid on the dustbin when I tell you! In the mean time, Big Trill – Pick!'

'Pick, WonderMax!'

Oh . . . gee whiz! Mumzie and everyone are climbing over fences.

Clambering through the house –

SMASH!

CRASH!

TRAMPLE!

Pick – throw!

Pick – throw!

Pick – throw!

'DANCE! DANCE! DANCE!'

'Back – all of you!' yells Little Trill, air freshener in one hand, dustbin lid (held like a shield) in the other. 'Back – or you get air-freshened!'

Still they move forward.

SMASH!

CRASH!

TRAMPLE!

'Hurry, Big Trill! Hurry! Just seven more flowers left. One . . . two . . . gee whiz! They're in the garden! Fire, Little Trill! Fire!'

'AIR FRESHENER AWAY!' cries Little Trill, and – aiming it at Mumzie –

Spraaayyy!

**04:13**
'Dance! Darling! – Oooo! What's that? Magnolia . . .' And for a moment, the new aroma surprises her. She stands still, dazed, blinking. But then . . . 'DANCE! DANCE! DANCE!'

'Good golly Miss Molly! It only holds them off for a second!'

'But it might give us those extra few seconds we need, Little Trill! Keep spraying! There's only five flowers to go . . .'

'DANCE, SHORT –'

Spraaayyy!

'OOOO! WHAT'S THAT?'

## 04:14

Pick!

Throw!

Four flowers left.

Pick!

Throw!

Three!

## 04:15

'Dance, Little Huck –'

Spray!

'Mercy! What's going on?'

Pick!

Throw!

Two!

## 04:16

'Blooming dance, Maxie –'

Spray!

'Ooo-errr! Luverducks!'

Pick!

Throw!

One!

**04:17**

'Dance, MAXie-WEE –'
    Spray!
        'eeEEE! WhAT'S up ME noSE now?'
        'Gee whiz! This last flower's on the end of the top branch . . . It's quite a stretch . . .'
'Careful, WonderMax!'
'Careful, WonderMax!'


**04:18**

Pick!
    Throw!
    'That's it! Quick, Little Trill! Slam the lid on!'
    Slam!
    'Now . . . Big Trill! Help me down! That's it! I'm gonna sit on the dustbin – Keep spraying, Little Trill! I want to smell nothing but magnolia!'
    Spraaaaayyyyyy!
    Spraaaaayyyyyy!
    Spraaaaayyyyyy!


**04:19**

'It's working, Big 'n' Little Trills!'
    'Oh, look at me, darling! Outside! In my

nightdress and – oh, lordy-lordy! I'm covered in twigs and leaves and – Oh, darling! What on earth got into me?'

'AND ME!'

'Mercy! Me too!'

'Luverducks! Me too!'

'mE TOo!'

And everyone starts murmuring amongst themselves, looking very embarrassed and confused.

'Darling! Give me a hug!'

Max rushes into his Mumzie's arms.

## 04:20

'Good golly Miss Molly! Looks like I can get rid of this thing!' declares Little Trill, removing the peg from his nose. 'At last! I can breathe properly!'

And then –

CRASH!

'Gee whiz – What's that? Oh no! Look! Baby Fleur's got to her feet and – she's knocked the dustbin over! The flowers are everywhere. And all I can smell is –'

'Chocolate!' cries Little Trill. 'Oh, what a foolish old man I've been! Forgive me, everyone! I've been keeping him from you. But now I realize the error of my ways, WonderMax – Dance! AND DANCE NOWWW!'

**04:21**
'DARLING – DANCE!'
   'SHORT STUFF – DANCE!'
   'LITTLE HUCK – DANCE!'
   'MAXIE – DANCE!'
   'MAXie-wEED – DanCE!'
   'WONDERMAX – DANCE!'
   'NOOOOOOOOOOOOOOOO!' cries Max. 'IT'S STARTING ALL OVER AGAIN, BIG TRILL – WHATEVER YOU DO, KEEP YOUR NOSE PEGGED!'

'Heavens to Betsy, yes, WonderMax! Oh, look at Brother Little Trill. He's glaring like a wild animal. If only your little sister hadn't –'

'We can't blame her, Big Trill. She's just a little baby –'

'WAAARGH!'

'And – oh, gee whiz – she's getting scared again! Oh, come here, Baby Fleur! Brother Max'll protect you! There, there! Don't cry – Don't cry!'

'WONDERMAX!' yells Little Trill, grabbing hold of Max's shoulder, 'DANCE THIS VERY

INSTANT! I'M YEARNING FOR IT! I'M CRAVING IT! I NEEEEED IT!'

**04:23**

'Unhand him, Brother Little Trill!' cries Big Trill, grabbing Max's other shoulder. 'The precious young fellow shall not dance! It is late! He is tired! And his shoes are giving him blisters –'

'OH SHUT UP, BOSSY BOOTS!' yells Little Trill.

'Little Trill!' gasps Big Trill. 'Wh-what are you saying? This is me! Your dear twin brother –'

'YEAH, BOSSY BOOTS! I'M FED UP WITH LISTENING TO YOU TELLING ME WHAT TO DO! WONDERMAX'S MUMZIE'S RIGHT! YOU *ARE* A BORING OLD FART! NOW LET GO OF THE KID! HE'S GONNA DANCE, OR MY NAME'S NOT TRILLIAN GEEZER!'

**04:25**

'Never, Little Trill! Now – you let go of the precious fellow. Because, I assure you, he is *not* going to dance, or *my* name's not Trillian Geezer either!'

'HE DOESN'T BELONG TO YOU!' Little Trill tugs at Max's shoulder. 'HE BELONGS TO ME!'

'Nonsense!' Big Trill tugs at Max's shoulder. 'He belongs to me!'

'HE BELONGS TO ME!' Tug!

'He belongs to me!' Tug!

'WAAARGH!'

'Stop it, Big 'n' Little Trills! Stop it! I'm holding Baby Fleur –'

'HE'S MINE!' Tug!

'HE'S MINE!' Tug!

'STOP IT! YOU'LL HURT BABY FLEUR! I'LL DANCE! YOU HEAR ME? I'LL DAAANNNCE!'

**04:27**
'But, WonderMax . . .' splutters Big Trill. 'You'll never be able to dance enough to please them. They'll just demand more and more –'

'No choice, Big Trill! I'm afraid for Baby Fleur. For her, I'll dance till there's blisters on my blisters.'

'DANCE! DANCE! DANCE!'

**04:29**
'Gee whiz! They're pulling me outside now, Big Trill. They want me to perform in the Square! Of course – not enough room for everyone to see me here! Careful, everyone! I'm holding a baby! Wait! I've got an idea! Big Trill – Where are you?'

'Here, my precious fellow!'

'Listen, Big Trill – Oh, gee whiz! I should have thought of it earlier! You've got to phone ZinderZunder!'

'Wh-who?'

'ZinderZunder! I can't phone again because I've already done it once! But you – you can do it! Just pick up the phone when we've left the house. You don't need a number. Just say, "ZinderZunder". You got that?'

'ZinderZunder?'

'That's it, Big Trill. Tell him what's going on. Say I need help – Argh! They're lifting me on to their shoulders now! Careful, everyone! Careful! I'm holding a baby! There, Baby Fleur – don't worry!

All safe! – BIG TRILL! DON'T FORGET! PHONE! SAY "ZINDERZUNDER"! GET HELP! JUST MAKE SURE YOU SAY IT WITH EVERY BIT OF PASSION IN YOUR HEART! AND HURRRYYY!'

**04:34**
I'm in the middle of the Square now! Still holding Baby Fleur! I won't let go of her, no matter what happens. My arms are the only safe place.

Look at everyone! All round me! Aiming torches like a hundred spotlights. Some are climbing trees to get a better look. Others are on rooftops. Or hanging out of windows.

WEOWEOWEOWEOWEOWEOWEOWEOW!

What's that?

Gee whiz! A police car!

WEOWEOWEOW!

Another one!

But as soon as the police get out and smell the flowers –

'DANCE! DANCE! DANCE!'

And look! The police are standing on top of their cars! Stamping their feet.

Oh, hurry up, Big Trill! Make that phone call!

'DANCE! DANCE! DANCE! DANCE! DANCE!'

**04:36**
Tap!

Tap!

Tap!

Ouch! My feet hurt so much! And my legs are more wobbly than ever –

TAP!

TAP!

TAP!

TAP!

TAPPITY!

Tap!

Tap!

**04:37**
The crowd is cheering!
    Cheering me on!
But – ouch – my poor feet!

TAP!

TAP!

Click!

Tippity!

Tap!

TIPPITY!  **TAP!**

*Spin!*

*Spin!*  *Tap!*

'Don't worry, Baby Fleur! I'll keep it gentle! No choice! Shoes really digging into my heels! I've got to have a rest . . .'

'DON'T STOP, DARLING!'

'WANT MORE, SHORT STUFF!'

'KEEP TAPPING, LITTLE HUCK!'

'LOTS BLOOMING MORE, MAXIE!'

'muCH More, MAxie-weED!'

'ENCORE, WONDERMAX! ENCORE! ENCORE!'

*Tap!*

*Tap!*

**Spin!**

*Tap!*

**04:40**

Tap!

Tap!

Tap!

At last! There's Big Trill! Fighting his way towards me.

'Big Trill! Big Trill –'

Tap!

Tappity!

'– did you get through?'

'Heavens to Betsy, yes, WonderMax!'

'Oh, razzmatazz news! ZinderZunder's sending help, I suppose –'

'ZinderZunder? My precious fellow, I didn't phone ZinderZunder!'

**04:41**

'But – why, Big Trill – Oh, no! No! Big Trill! YOUR NOSE IS DE-PEGGED!'

'Slipped off, my precious fellow. On the way to your house! And that's when I realized the true error of my ways! What a fool I've been to stop you dancing! You're a genius! And the whole world should know it! So I phoned the local TV station! They're sending reporters and cameras! I'm so proud of you, WonderMax! We both are, aren't we, Brother Little Trill?'

'Indeedy yes, Brother Big Trill.'

'And soon – the whole world will see what our precious fellow can do! Oh, heavens to Betsy – DANCE, WONDERMAX! I NEED IT! I NEED IT!'

And, once again, the rest of the crowd picks up the chant. Only this time it is louder than ever . . .

## 'DANCE! DANCE! DANCE!'

**04:43**

'Oh, gee whiz! I'm sorry, Baby Fleur! There's no help coming! I . . . d-don't know what to do! Will you ever forgive me?'

TAP!           **TAP!**

Tap!

Tap!           Tap!

**04:45**

'Oh, you're smiling at me, Baby Fleur . . . Thank you . . . You're my only friend now . . . In the whole world . . . Only you . . . Ouch! Gee whiz! My blisters, Baby Fleur. My feet hurt so much. Look at me! Wobbling all over the place . . .'

TAP!

TAP!

TAP!

TAP!

Tap!

CLICK!

**04:46**

'This is the worst dancing I've ever done, Baby Fleur. But . . . look at everyone. They're loving it . . . No matter what I do . . . They whoop and cheer . . . Ouch! Ouch! And look! Television cameras! And reporters! And look! A helicopter circling above!'

TAP!

Tappity!

TAP!

TIP!

Spin!
Spin!

Tappity!

Tap!

**04:48**

'Oh, Baby Fleur! I'm so, so . . . tired . . . Only you keep me going . . . I love you, Baby Fleur!'

TAP!

Tappity!

Tap!

'Oh, I can't carry on, Baby Fleur. I just can't. Why won't someone help me . . . Help me, someone . . . For my sister's sake . . . HELLLPPP!'

**04:50**

ZMMMMMMMMMM.

'Wh-what's that noise, Baby Fleur? Can you hear it? A low humming. So low, my bones are vibrating.'

ZMMMMMMMMMM.

'Getting louder! Where's it coming from? Everywhere?'

ZMMMMMMMMMM.

'Gee whiz! A light! Like sunrise! But it can't be sunrise yet – Oh, look! It *can't* be! Baby Fleur, look up! It's bigger than the whole Square. And it's as bright as the sun! And smaller lights are flashing round it! IT'S A FLYING SAUCER, BABY FLEUR! IT'S A UFO!'

ZMMMMM –

   Then silence!

   Everyone staring up!

   Motionless.

   Well, gee whiz, I suppose if anything's going to surprise them enough to stop chanting 'DANCE!' it's a flying saucer –

   Cha-chonk!

   A tiny, circular door's opened at the bottom of the craft. Difficult to see clearly – everything's glowing so bright –

   Shpoo – shpoo – shpoo –

   What's that? Look! A rope ladder's being

thrown out of the door. It's unwinding all the way
to the ground –

Shpoo – shpoo –

Best step back! Looks like it's gonna land right
next to me –

Shpop!

There!

## 04:55

'Awfully sorry about the delay, everyone,' says a
voice inside the flying saucer. 'Blasted anti-gravity
tele-porter broke yesterday! Dashed nuisance!
Can't quite work out how to navigate this ladder!
Won't be a jiffy! Amuse yourselves while you're
waiting!'

That . . . that must be ZinderZunder. Doesn't
sound anything like he did on the phone! As I
thought – a voice distorter was being used.

'Nearly there, everyone! Can't apologize
enough! Just getting my balance! Damned
tricky . . .'

And then . . .

A foot!

## 04:56

There he is! Making his way down the ladder! He's
right – it does look tricky. Swaying backwards and
forwards like that.

'Aha! Getting my rhythm now, everyone! Soon
be with you! Don't go away! Dashed wobbly
though.'

Look at him! He's wearing neat, polished shoes.
A neat, pinstriped suit with a flower in the

buttonhole. A bowler hat. And . . . an umbrella's hanging from one arm! No wonder the ladder's difficult for him. Still – he's made it down!

'Aha! Spiffing! Now then – Max Huckabee, I presume.'

## 04:57

'Er . . . indeedy, yes.'

'Pleasure to meet you, old chap. Oh, don't bother shaking hands! You keep a grip on the little mite. Baby Fleur, is it? Charming! Quite charming! A little angel. Although, of course, most angels tend to smell of bread pudding at this age, don't they?'

'Gee whiz! I really d-don't know. Am I right in thinking you're ZinderZunder?'

'Stars 'n' garters! Where's my manners! Left them in the Arctic with my silver toothpick, I shouldn't wonder. Yes, yes, yes, old chap, Zinder-Zunder at your service. Although, please, I beg you, call me Mr Zed! Everyone does. Except the Abominable Snowman, of course. But then you know how irritable they get with all that fur. Lousy with fleas you know!'

'Mr Zed . . . can you help?'

'Help? My dear chap – that's why I'm here! And, by the looks of it, just in the nick of time! Would have been here sooner, of course, but there's problems all over the place tonight –'

'Dance! Dance! Dance!'

'Mr Zed! Look! The novelty of the spacecraft is wearing off –'

'It's a ZinderZunder Everywhere Anytime

Vehicle to be precise, dear chap. Or a ZEAV to use the current jargon –'

'DANCE! DANCE! DANCE!'

'Stars 'n' garters! I see what you mean. The natives are restless tonight.' Mr Zed looks up and calls, 'RIBA!'

And the next second –

**04:59**

– a bird flies out of the craft. It swoops down to Mr Zed.

'That's the bird!' cries Max. 'The one that rapped on my window and –'

'Brought you the ZinderZunderseed! Spot on, old chap. It's also the bird that stayed around to see what happened, then reported back to yours truly. Oh, I know what you're going to say: You never saw it. Of course you didn't. ZinderZunderbirds are highly skilled at camouflage. A million of them could sneak up on you and you wouldn't know it till they pecked your nose. Now excuse me, old chap! Got to have a word in ZunderZunderbirdeze.'

And, talking directly to the bird, Mr Zed goes on, 'Tik da toc toc! Tic! Tic! Nyan nyo yo hi! Moni da tic doo!'

The bird flies back to the craft.

'Gee whiz! Wh-what did you tell it?'

'You'll see, old chap.'

And the very next second –

**05:00**

– the bird flies out again, followed by seven others.

Each one is holding a gas mask in its beak.

'I've instructed them to give a gas mask to your immediate family and friends, old chap,' Mr Zed explains. 'Max, allow me to introduce you to the other birds. The one giving your Mumzie a gas mask is Zooba. The one giving your Daddy Rosco a mask is Skiba. Granny Blossom, Feeby. Aunt Kiki, Tonko. Cousin Otis, Bik-Bik. Big Trill, Shoshka. Little Trill, Finto.'

'You seem to know everyone here, Mr Zed! Is there anything you don't know?'

'Well, the winner of the nineteen seventy-two Eurovision Song Contest seems to elude me at the moment. But apart from that, yes – I believe I *do* know everything! Aha! You see! The masks have calmed them down. They're regaining their senses!'

'But what about the rest, Mr Zed? Look at them! They're still –'

'DANCE! DANCE! DANCE!'

'– and there's no time to give out thousands of gas masks.'

'Give out more gas masks? Stars 'n' garters, old chap, I had no intention of doing that! Your family and friends get masks because I need to talk to them. As for the rest . . . well, that's simple – STOP, EVERYONE, IF YOU PLEASE!'

## 05:02

And they did stop.

Every one of them.

In fact, they froze.

Gee whiz! It's like a video on 'pause'. Look!

There's someone who was jumping out of a tree –
stuck in mid-air! And someone else running –
perched on the toes of one foot. And look! That
dog! It's in the middle of barking – its mouth open,
tongue out.

'There,' sighs Mr Zed. 'A little peace and quiet
at last, eh? Now, Max, old chap, perhaps you'll
introduce me to our gas-masked brethren.'

'But you know who they are!'

'My dear chap, I need a *formal* introduction, if you please. Where are your manners?'

## 05:04

'Mr Zed, this is my Mumzie.'

'Enchanted, dear lady.' Mr Zed takes Mumzie's hand and kisses it graciously.

'Mmffmm – Mmffmm! Humff-immff moffmm-umppff,' Mumzie mumbles through the gas mask.

'My dear lady, please, don't give it another thought,' says Mr Zed, obviously understanding every muffled syllable. 'Of *course* I haven't caught you at your best! Although, I must say, the foliage in your hair does give you a certain dramatic quality.'

'Mr Zed, this is my Daddy Rosco.'

'Pleasure, sir, pleasure.' Mr Zed shakes Daddy Rosco's hand vigorously.

'HMFF HMFF YMMFF YMMFF UMMFFY UMMMM!'

'Stars 'n' garters, yes, my dear sir, my ZEAV must take a lot of polishing. But, as you probably know, this is the latest model and it has a self-washing 'n' polishing device and, believe me, I use it quite often.'

'Mr Zed . . . this is Granny Blossom!'

'An honour and a privilege, madam.' Kiss hand.

'HUMFY! EMMPPHY! EMPHY!'

'My dear madam, please do not be embarrassed by anything. I've seen more large ladies in their nightclothes than you've had after-dinner mints. And, I do assure you, they have a beauty equal to that of Helen of Troy, who – I hasten to add – was partial to the odd custard cream herself.'

'Mr Zed . . . my Aunt Kiki!'

'Charmed, madam.' Kiss.

Aunt Kiki is speechless.

'My Cousin Otis.'

'Good to see you, young chap! Stars 'n' garters! What a firm grip you have. Reminds me of Hercules when he was your age.'

'HUMffmm imFUNN immMMY UMPff.'

'Did I *know* Hercules? My dear chap, I taught him all he knew.'

'And, Mr Zed, this is Big Trill and Little Trill!'

'My dear, dear chaps! What a thrill to meet you!' Shake! Shake! 'I haven't seen you since . . . Oh, when was it? The summer of nineteen fifty-two. You were performing at the Empire Ballroom.'

'Umffy umffy yunn umpff.'

'Umffy umffy yunn umpff!'

'Oh yes, I'm a great fan of music hall. I often drop in on the acts I admire. Middle of the front row, that's where you'll find me. Best seat in the house. And, Mr Trillian Geezer and Mr Trillian Geezer, may I tell you that your tap-dancing was every bit as entertaining as . . . well, the night Merlin performed dressage on Pegasus round the turrets of Camelot.'

'Merlin!' gasps Max. 'You actually *knew* Merlin!'

'*Knew* him!' chuckles Mr Zed. 'Why, my dear chap, Merlin was one of the first recipients of a ZinderZundertree!'

**05:10**

'Gee whiz . . . it's a shame the ZinderZundertree you sent me didn't work as well as Merlin's –'

'Wow! Slow down, old chap! Let's get one thing perfectly clear before we go any further. It was not – repeat: *not* – me who sent you the ZinderZundertree.'

'But . . . but I spoke to you on the phone –'

'No, old chap, you didn't! Stars 'n' garters! There's an explanation due, dear chap. And you'll get it, I assure you. Tell you what – why don't I go and have a natter with your family and friends for a while – Mumzie! Can we go to your humble abode? Perhaps you can make us all a nice pot of tea.'

'Umffy! Un Umffy Umpf!'

'Splendid! And now, Max, old chap,' Mr Zed continues, 'while I'm doing that – you can talk to the person responsible for this whole ghastly palaver.' He looks up at the ZEAV once more and calls, 'ZINNIE! COME DOWN AND APOLOGIZE! STOP HIDING, YOU BOUNDER! ZINNIE! ZINNIE!'

**05:14**

Look! Someone else is climbing down the ladder . . . Gee whiz! It's a boy. About my age . . . He's wearing trainers and jeans – both quite scruffy. And a baggy T-shirt! And – geee whiiizzz! – his hair! What a long, tangly mop! It's covering the boy's face!

'Oh, do buck up, Zinnie,' Mr Zed calls. 'A little vim and vinegar, if you please.' Then he glances at Max and continues, 'Zinnie's such a lazy scoundrel. Not like you, old chap – Aha! There you are, Zinnie, old chap. Now please don't slouch like that. And – stars 'n' garters! – take that hair out of your face. It's like looking at the Woolly Mammoth of Borneo.'

Zinnie's sighing! Gee whiz – what a deep sigh. He's obviously heard this a million times before – Now he's parting his hair! Not much. Just enough to look at me with one heavy-lidded, drowsy eye.

'Max, old chap,' says Mr Zed brightly, 'may I introduce my son, Zinnie.'

'Your son? Gee whiz!'

'And Zinnie, old chap – this is Max! Who you owe an apology to. And while you're doing that, I shall go into Mumzie's house and enjoy her hospitality. I say, Max, old chap, why don't you give me Baby Fleur. Give your arms a rest while you natter to Zinnie!'

'But –'

'It's perfectly safe, old chap. I'll give her straight to your Mumzie to look after. You can trust me. She's safe now. Honestly.'

Carefully, Max puts Baby Fleur in Mr Zed's arms. 'She's watching everything, Mr Zed. Look – she's smiling at you!'

'What a spiffing angel she is!' Mr Zed sighs. 'Now – Zinnie, you scoundrel! Explain your dastardly behaviour. See you in a tick, old chaps.'

## 05:16

'Gee whiz!' says Max, watching Mr Zed and the others go indoors. 'It must be . . . well, pure razzmatazz to have a dad like that. I mean . . . he is a wizard or something, right?'

'No fooling you, is there?'

'Well, I don't know why you're in such a grumpy mood. It's me who's had a totally horrific night. And look – *I'm* not grumpy! In fact, I'm feeling quite . . . what's the word? Exhilarated! That's it! Well – gee whiz – it's not every day I see all my neighbours frozen like they are now. Look at them! Fascinating!'

'Oh, *really*? You find it *fascinating*, do you?'

'Well . . . indeedy, yes. Gee whiz! Don't you?'

'Listen – as far as I'm concerned – everything's

boring. You hear me? BOOORRRING! You're as bad as Dad. He finds everything fascinating too. Know what he bought me as a pet? A unicorn!'

'Fascinati –'

'They're not, dingbat! Unicorns are the most BOOORRRING animals ever created! Playing with them's about as interesting as watching paint dry. Same as dragons – BOOORRRING! And as for dinosaurs – oh, PERRR-LEEEZE! They haven't got the sense of a lettuce leaf! But Dad, he won't stop! Every day another BOOORRRING present. Know what it was yesterday? Excalibur.'

'Ex-Excalibur! You mean. . . the *sword*?'

'Nah, Excalibur the draught-excluder – Course I mean the sword, you dingbat! Dad invited the Lady of the Lake over for tea and biscuits.'

'And she . . . *gave* you Excalibur.'

'Well, I didn't *steal* it, if that's what you're getting at!'

'Oh, indeedy, no! But surely, Excalibur must be fascin –'

'Gimme a break! What good's Excalibur to me? Big clumpy thing. Can't even cut worms up with it – BOOORRRING! And when I complain to Dad – what does he do? He gives me a Zesty Dung Wrangler!'

'What's a Zesty Dung Wrangler?'

'Well . . . put it this way – Zesty Dung Wranglers make unicorns look interesting!'

**05:18**

Max chuckles, 'You've got a good sense of humour, Zinnie.'

'You . . . you think so?'

'Well, you make me laugh.'

'Shucks – thanks! And . . . well, I'm sorry for all the trouble I caused. You see, what happened was –'

'Don't tell me, Zinnie! I can guess. You were bored. So, when your dad wasn't looking, you sent out the ZinderZundergram. Right?'

'Yeah . . . right.'

Max puts his arm round Zinnie's shoulder. 'Gee whiz, Zinnie! You know something? If I was bored, I'd have done exactly the same thing!'

Zinnie parts his hair even more, revealing a wide grin.

'You would, Max?'

'I would, Zinnie.'

And for a moment, the two boys smile at each other.

Then –

'Zinnie! We can't leave all the neighbours like this! How do we get things . . . well, back to normal?'

'Easy, Max! Take me to the ZinderZundertree.'

## 05:19

'Gee whiz! It looks even bigger! Look at it! Way above the rooftops now.'

'Yeah, you must have got an extra-large seed. Usually, they're only half this size. Yours ain't the largest though. Cleopatra had one three times taller.'

'Cleopatra had a ZinderZundertree?'

'Well, actually, she had two.'

'How come?'

'She flirted with Dad and – well, say no more, eh? And don't tell Dad I told you. He's a little embarrassed by the whole thing.'

'My lips are sealed, Zin – Look! The tree's still growing! Quick! How do I stop it?'

'Simple-pimple! Just reverse what you did before – How many times did you have to say your five-word wish?'

'Nineteen.'

'So now you've got to say it *backwards* nineteen times!'

## 05:21

'Gee whiz! I don't think I even *know* what it *is* backwards.'

'Zzatamzzar ym gid tsum enoyreve.'

'H-how did you work that out so quickly?'

'I'm a wizard's son! What can I say?'

## 05:22

Max gets to his knees and, very carefully, starts to whisper at the roots of the tree, 'Zzatamzzar ym gid –'

'Got to be faster than that, Max.'

'But it's difficult, Zin.'

'No one said magic's easy. You remember the rules: "very fast and without a break". Go on! Go for it!'

## 05:23

'Zzatamzzarymgidtsumenoyrevezzatamzzarymgidtsumenoyrevezzatamzzarymgidtsumenoyrevezzatamzzarymgidtsumenoyrevezzatamzzarymgidtsumenoyrevezzatamzzarymgidtsumenoyrevezzatamzzarymgidtsumenoyrevezzatamzzarymgidtsumenoyrevezzatamzzarymgidtsumenoyrevezzatamzzarymgidtsumenoyrevezzatamzzarymgidtsumenoyrevezzatamzzarymgidtsumenoyrevezzatamzzarymgidtsumenoyrevezzatamzzarymgidtsumenoyrevezzatamzzarymgidtsumenoyreve!'

## 05:24

'Well done, Max!' says Zinnie. 'And – there – look! The tree's starting to ungrow!'

Gee whiz! Look! The flowers are closing –

Sssssiwq!

Sssssiwq!

Sssssiwq!

– And now the branches and twigs are shrinking! Gee whiz! Like film in reverse!

The tree's getting smaller!

Smaller!

Smaller!

Now it's my height!

Up to my chest!

Waist!

Knees!

Ankles!

It's a green shoot again!

And then –

'IT'S GONE, ZIN!'

## 05:26

'Now finish it off, Max! – Dig it up!'

'Oh – gee whiz! Indeedy, yes!'

Scrape the earth away! Glad it's no deeper than my little finger – Ah! There it is. Give it to Zin –

'Not me, Max! Give it back to the bird – RIBA! RIBA!'

And the next second, the bird swoops from the sky and –

'It's taken it from me!'

'It's over, Max!'

**05:27**

'Well, not quite, Zin – Look! Through the kitchen window. Mr Zed is still talking to Mumzie and Daddy Rosco and Granny Blossom and Aunt Kiki and Cousin Otis. Gee whiz! They're listening very hard! And look! They're taking their gas masks off now! Mr Zed must have told them it's safe. Look! Birds are swooping in through the broken windows and taking the masks back! What razzmatazz animals those birds are! And look at Baby Fleur in Mumzie's arms –'

'Babies are BOOORRRIN –'

'They're not boring, Zin! At least, Baby Fleur's not. Her little hands held me. She smiled at me. She needs me. She's not boring at all. Indeedy, no! She's . . . pure razzmatazz! – Look! Mr Zed's standing up now! And . . . gee whiz! Everyone else is leaving. Mumzie and Daddy Rosco are going upstairs. What's happening? Quick! Let's go to Mr Zed!'

**05:31**

'Aha! There you are, old chaps! Well, I've had an absolutely spiffing chat with your family. What charming chappies. Especially your mother, Max, old chap. Reminds me a little of a mermaid I once knew. Mermaids are dashed house-proud creatures too, you know. Always polishing their conch shells. Stars 'n' garters! Look at the time! Really must be going! Why don't you walk me and Zinnie back to the ZEAV, old chap!'

'But – where are they going, Mr Zed? Mumzie and Daddy –'

'Oh, don't fret, old chap. Sent them all off to bed. Good forty winks'll do them the world of good! And don't worry about Baby Fleur – your mermaid-like Mumzie'll put her in her cot –'

'But it's crushed, Mr Zed! The cot! My neighbours trampled –'

'Don't get in a tizz, old chap! The ZinderZunderbirds will have seen to all that by now – Come outside! You'll see what I mean.'

**05:34**

Look at the birds! Flying around so fast they're nothing but multicoloured blurs. And everywhere they fly, things get mended.

— 132 —

What magic!

Crushed flowers are uncrushed.

Trampled bushes are untrampled.

Broken fences are unbroken.

Smashed windows are unsmashed.

The birds are mending the Square. Pretty soon it'll be back to normal. As if nothing happened. But what about –

'The people, Mr Zed! Look at them! They're still frozen!'

'Stars 'n' garters! I knew I'd forgotten something – TIME FOR BED, OLD CHAPS! NIGHTY-NIGHT!'

Everyone's moving now. Like they're sleep-walking.

Going back to their beds.

Calmly.

Peacefully.

Police cars driving away.

Helicopters flying off.

Film-crews dispersing.

And the ZinderZunderbirds are whizzing round them all.

Torn clothes are untorn.

Scratched skin is unscratched.

Leaves and twigs are plucked from hair.

'The ZinderZunderbirds will be finished before you know it, old chap,' says Mr Zed with pride. 'By the time you get back home, everything will be exactly as it was before any of this happened. And no one will remember. Not a single thing . . . Except you.'

**05:37**

'You mean . . . everyone will forget what happened tonight, Mr Zed?'

'But, of course, old chap! Can't have everyone knowing about me! That would never do. So – by morning – all memory and record of this night will be gone. Stars 'n' garters! Look at the time. Really must fly. Don't think you were the only None Too Happy Young Person to receive one of Zinnie's dashed ZinderZundergrams, Max, old chap! There's a place – not a million miles from here – where a tree is growing Zorillas! And you know what a dashed mess a rampant Zorilla can cause. Oh, one more thing, old chap! That talk I had with your family . . . I planted a few – how shall I say? – thoughts! Not brainwashing or magic. Just suggested they try to see your side of it a bit more. So you might see a little difference in the future. But, if you don't mind me saying so, old chap, you should see *their* side too.'

**05:39**

'*Their* side?' gasps Max. 'But . . . what *is* their side?'

'Oh, stars 'n' garters, don't get all in a tizz again. I know you're upset by them not appreciating your dancing. But you should . . . well, search your heart for your own – how shall I say? – intolerance, perhaps. How much did *you* . . . well, get interested in *them*? In Daddy Rosco's car, for example. Or Cousin Otis's muscles. And as for Aunt Kiki – can you honestly say you never looked down your nose at her? And as for Mumzie – that charming mermaid-creature – she needs you to be interested in *her* life, as well as *her* being interested in *yours*. And a big part of her new life is . . .'

'Baby Fleur! Oh, Mr Zed – what's happened tonight. All of this. Gee whiz! Perhaps there's a message –'

'Message!?' cries Mr Zed in total disgust. 'I certainly hope not, old chap. If I want a message, I'll buy an answerphone.

Now, it's been a pleasure meeting you, Max. I'll leave you two boys alone to say your farewells. Don't be long, Zinnie! Some mischievous Zorillas need our attention before morning!'

And with that, Mr Zed climbs up the ladder.

**05:41**

'It's been razzmatazz meeting you, Zin.'

'Likewise, Max.'

'Wish we could have talked for longer! I've got a tap-dancing routine I'd love to show you.'

'And I've got some CDs I'd like to play you.'

'What kind of music do you like?'

'Heavy metal! You like heavy metal?'

'I'm not sure. Can you tap-dance to it?'

'Well, you could try –'

'ZINNIE! A LITTLE VIM AND VINEGAR, IF YOU PLEASE! A LITTLE VIM AND VINEGAR!'

'I've got to go, Max. I think I'm going to play my heavy metal extra loud tonight!'

'Will I ever see you again?'

'I hope so.'

## 05:43

'Zin! Can you do one thing for me? Ask your dad . . . well, ask him to change his mind about making *everyone* forget what happened? It'll be so lonely! Me being the only one. No one to share the memory. Even if it's just one person, Zin. Just one?'

'I'll ask him, Max. But he never listens to me.'

'He might!'

'ZINNIE!'

'Bye, Max.'

'A most razzmatazz goodbye, Zin.'

## 05:45

Gone!

Zin and Mr Zed have gone.

I'm standing in the Square – alone.

Smell of flowers.

Bird calls.

So peaceful –

'WAAARGHHH!'

'Baby Fleur!'

## 05:47

I'm rushing into the house now. Up the stairs!

Look! Everything is mended. Magic.

Into Baby Fleur's room.

There she is! Tucked up in her cot.

'Don't cry, Baby Fleur. Brother Max is here.'

I kiss her gently.

She stops crying.

And then –

'Goo . . . ga . . .'

She's trying to say something!

I kiss her again. Then walk towards the door.
I'm so tired.

And then –

'Goo . . . ga . . . Zin . . . Zun . . .'

## 05:48

I turn and stare at Baby Fleur.

Zin . . . Zun . . . ZinderZunder! She's trying to
say ZinderZunder! That means –

Zinnie did it! He persuaded Mr Zed to change
his mind. One person will remember.

My sister!

'Oh, Baby Fleur! What times we'll have when
you grow up! We'll talk and talk. The secrets we'll
share. We'll be the best friends in the whole world.'

Oh – gee whiz! – the best razzmatazz is yet to
come.

## 06:00

Max is in bed now. Look at him. Exactly as he was
when the day began. Tucked up and dreaming . . .

And what is he dreaming?

Well, he's on a stage. And dancing. But this
time, he's not alone.

It's some years in the future and Baby Fleur can tap-dance every bit as well as her brother.

Above the stage a million neon lights declare, 'THE HUCKABEES – THE GREATEST TAP-DANCERS THE COSMOS HAS EVER KNOWN!'

And in the audience, Mumzie, Daddy Rosco, Granny Blossom, Aunt Kiki and Cousin Otis whoop and cheer.

## 06:01

And as I told you, this story has taken exactly one day to tell.

In a little while daffodils, tulips and hyacinths will turn their colourful blooms towards the dawn. Butterflies and bees will flutter and buzz from petal to nectar.

Oh yes, there will be –

## 06:02

– light: yellow and orange.

The sound of birds.

And you'll smell – flowers.

Because it will be –

## 06:03

Sunrise.